A DEATH WORTH LIVING

TREY STONE

I dedicate this book to myself, who I've been and who I've become.

This is a collection of fictional works. Names, characters, places, and incidents are either a product of the author's imagination or are used fictitiously. Any resemblance to actual persons, living or dead, businesses, companies, events, or locales, is entirely coincidental.

A Death Worth Living

Inked in Gray Press

InkedinGray.com

Cover Design by Squidblot Arts

Foreword

This is a work of fiction. At the same time, it's the most personal book I've ever written. In fact – it's all about me. It's heavily based on my childhood, my early years at school, and the place I grew up. All the characters are real. That is, they are based on real people. My mother, father, siblings. Every single one.

I didn't set out to write this book like this, like a personal self-exploration, but I'm very glad I did. It . . . well, for the lack of a better word, let's just say it did the trick.

Thank you, for sharing this story with me. I hope maybe you can find what I found in it.

That Time I Died

I was dead at twenty. After just two measly decades, at the height of my prime, I was robbed of what I can only assume would have been a long and wonderful life.

And it was the best thing to ever happen to me. Let me tell you why.

My name's Jacob, born Jacob Terrance Royce, the middle son of two loving parents who hated each other. One older sister, Nina, and a younger brother, Ford. Our parents divorced when I was ten. I was used to yelling at all of them, for all kinds of reasons, but I definitely yelled more at my parents after they tore our family to shreds, burned the scraps, and poured the ashes down the drain.

No, I'm not bitter.

I yelled at my sister mostly just for being a sister, which is probably the second most annoying category of person that exists, and I yelled at Ford a lot, usually just because he was around.

When I died, I had just turned twenty. Home for the

summer after my first year of college, working in my dad's friend's warehouse. I stacked boxes, moved stuff around, unpacked freight, and put things in the mail. I loved that job. Sounds pretty boring, I know, and it was! But that's exactly what made it awesome. I had the whole space to myself to rock out to tunes, and I could have as many coffee breaks as I wanted.

The warehouse sold and shipped parts, tech, and gizmos for suppliers of agricultural equipment. Think oil filters, gears, and drive belts for machines like tractors and combine harvesters. But we also had a shop in the front of the building where we sold the odd gardening tool, dog food, and hugely overpriced overalls. Honestly, the store-part of the warehouse was the ancient relic of the business that refused to die. We hardly ever had any customers in there, but the boss wouldn't give in and face the facts. Very occasionally, a real-life person would stop by the physical store like I'm told people used to do back in the day, have a look at some of our very dated merchandise without ever buying anything, and our boss would harrumph around all day, bellowing "I told you so!"

That day, I'd been asked to paint some display cases. My boss had gotten them cheap from some shop down the street, and his plan was to use them to showcase our newest line of last years' products. So, someone needed to paint them in our store colors, which were yellow and green.

"Fine," I said. How hard can painting be, right?

I imagine if I had seen it happen, I would have laughed. Not that death is funny, but the way I understand things happened sounds hilarious.

At one end of the warehouse, you have me, painting.

I had laid out some long rolls of packing paper along the back wall, where I had enough room to turn the cases as I painted each side, and where they wouldn't be in the way when I waited for the paint to dry.

At the other end, you have one of my colleagues, who — though he didn't work in the warehouse, only I did that — was driving a forklift. He had been asked to retrieve a pallet with some parts and stupidly said yes to get away from the stuff he was actually paid to do. He must have been directly opposite me in that big, cold hall full of shelves and boxes.

I, as any respectable at-the-cusp-of-his-teenage-years-year-old person did, was listening to music. Who wants to willingly expose themselves to the sounds of the universe when you can have *Iron Maiden* blasting through your ears? People say heavy metal is just indistinguishable noise, but to me, that's what everything else was.

To make a long and excruciatingly painful story short, my coworker crashed the forklift into our huge industrial shelves. One tipped over into the next, which tipped into the next . . . you get it.

I was at the end and, due to my fondness for making my eardrums bleed to the velvety sounds of Bruce Dickinson, I didn't hear the thing that crushed the life out of me.

I felt it though.

But only momentarily.

In hindsight, I realize my error, but in my defense, I'd always been alone in that warehouse. I never needed to be cautious. A lesson learned too late.

Eran

When I woke up, I felt hungover. Like I'd been out drinking all night — all weekend even — trying to win the gold medal in body shots.

My mouth was dry and sticky, and I can't say everything didn't ache like a bitch. The throbbing headache was the worst, but it all kind of washed away as soon as I saw *him*.

"Who are you?" I remember asking. It was the first thing to come into my head. To this day I can't think of why I started with that. I could have asked where I was, what had happened, or why they were staring at me, but none of that even grazed my mind.

He had the most intense crystal blue eyes I've ever seen. I'm not sure *blue* even describes them, but it's the only word I know that I think you'll understand. His hair was blonde, almost white, and though I know it was short, I can't picture what it actually looked like. The haircut he had escaped me, for some reason. Also, his skin was white. And I'm not talking about the kind of beige color you might imagine when you think of a person having white skin. I'm talking paper-white. Like snow. It was unnerving for a moment, for a fleeting second, then the feeling dissipated. There was something calming about his appearance. Something tranquil about his presence in this strange place.

"Eran," he answered.

I keep saying *he*, and I feel like I need to clear something up. I assume Eran was a man. But . . . let's just say their visage was very ambiguous, so I guess I can't be sure.

My dad and I watched a movie once where this woman played Bob Dylan. I can't remember the name. But Eran was kind of like that. They looked like they could be a woman. There was no beard, no hint of facial hair, though they could have been just clean-shaven. They were lithe and not too tall, and they had a pleasant face.

At the same time, there were none of those obvious features that would suggest they were a woman either. Maybe death was just . . . different.

It wasn't until after Eran introduced themselves that I realized I had woken up in a bed that wasn't my own. It was a plain room. As far as I can remember, I saw nothing on the walls, nothing around or behind Eran, or anything anywhere that would indicate where I was.

"Where am I?"

I don't know if I was expecting Eran to know, but seeing as they were there when I woke up, I assumed they did. They were there too, after all, and they were awake when *I* got there.

That's when they broke it to me: "You're dead."

The pain of my last moments came rushing back. It felt as if I was reliving a memory I'd had for forever. I shuddered, but weirdly enough, I believed them.

You would think that if someone came up to you saying you were dead, you would panic. Maybe scream and cry or be confused about what was going on. The six stages of grief come to mind, and you can imagine people being angry and denying it all.

But it wasn't like that. Honestly, my reaction was simple. "All right."

"You can get up if you want." Eran gestured to the side of the bed, inviting me to stand.

I threw the covers off, revealing that I was dressed underneath. Dark blue jeans and a *Pantera* t-shirt. My favorite outfit.

Swinging my legs out of the bed and hopping down on the tiled floor, I became very aware of how easy everything felt. How light and strong I was. Not a feeling I remember ever having. I felt so powerful. Until I turned around and saw myself lying there. I was on a bed, but not one I recognized. It's that classic, stepping-out-of-your-body cliché you see in movies. Both my parents were standing there, and for the first time since forever, they were holding each other. It was like they were identifying their dead son in a morgue, except the rest of the morgue wasn't there. It was just them, and me lying eyes closed on a plain white bed.

Dad had his arm wrapped around Mom's shoulder; she had hers around his waist, and they were crying. It was kind of beautiful were it not for the fact that their son was dead and half his skull was missing. (Thankfully, they didn't see the other part of my skull. At least I hope they hadn't.)

"Guess I really am dead," I said as I turned back to Eran. "And they can't see me?"

My parents weren't illusions. They weren't shadowy mirages or anything. They looked just like normal people, and as far as I could see, I was standing right next to them. Except I obviously wasn't, seeing as they didn't scream in horror at the sight of their ghostly son.

"No, they can't see you," Eran replied. Their voice was a certain but monotonous stream of words. Not excited, not timid, just a row of syllables, one after the other. "We can see them, and much of what goes on around them, but we're in no way there."

I would have argued if it wasn't obvious that Eran was right. "Are you God?"

That almost made them smile, I think. Eran didn't have any facial expression and didn't show much emotion at all during the time we were together actually, but I swear the corner of their mouth moved a bit. A noticeable bit.

"No, not at all. Sorry to disappoint."

I wasn't holding out much hope that they were, to be honest. In fact, judging by their whole demeanor, I'd probably be a bit disappointed if they were. If the almighty God — the creator of life, the universe, and everything that ever was — was just . . . a barely reactive Eran . . . yeah, that would have been weird.

"An angel then?"

For the first time since I had woken up, Eran moved, stepping closer to me while folding their hands behind his back.

"That might be an apt description actually. But not in the biblical sense, of course. If there is a God, and I mean at all, in any way, shape, or form, then I'm not aware of it. And I'm certainly not affiliated in any way. Think of me as a guide. You're dead now, and there are some things you have to do before you get to . . . ." Eran hesitated for a moment, and it sounded like their voice got caught in something. "Before you get to move on."

"So, this is the afterlife?" I was still kind of impressed with how chill I was. Not the slightest scared or angry — I wasn't even sad that I was dead. When you're a teenager with lots of bottled-up anxiety and anger towards the world, you find yourself imagining it all being over occasionally, and I got to say, I was impressed with how pleasant everything felt. All my worries were washed away. I felt lighter, freer even.

Eran shrugged. "It's a kind of afterlife, I guess."

"You guess? You mean you don't know?"

"I don't have all the answers, no. I'm sorry, Jacob."

"No, that's all right."

I turned to take in the sight of my parents again. They were still standing exactly like they had been, holding each other and crying as they looked down on my solemn body. It struck me that they hadn't even slightly moved at all. This wasn't a live feed I was looking at, then. It was a still moment, captured just as they embraced each other to mourn their dead son. I turned back to Eran, and I think I smiled for some reason.

"All right. Guide me."

Eran cast a glance over their shoulder, looking at a door behind them. I imagine that, had I known them, I would have been able to tell if they were nervous. If I had met them for longer than fifteen minutes, I would know what those facial expressions — or the lack of thereof — meant. But right then, I had no idea.

Were they nervous? Hell if I knew.

Were they going to tell me? I guessed not.

"Do you know why you died, Jacob?"

That made me shudder. The kind of cold jolt running down the length of your spine that forces you to shake your shoulders, hoping to drop that awful feeling.

Judgment, that's what it was.

When Eran asked me, it felt as if I was being judged by some higher being.

Even though I'd had time to ask Eran if they were either

God or an angel, I hadn't yet considered that they could be something else entirely.

You know, the other end of the scale, so to speak.

Should I be afraid? Could this creature be malevolent? All these thoughts rushed into my head and the cold around me made me—

"Neither do I," Eran said.

I realized I forgot to reply.

Eran smiled. "I'm sure we'll figure it out."

I frowned. "Will we?"

"Follow me."

Eran turned and began walking away. As my feet started moving to catch up, the hallway we were in stretched. Exactly like one of those cartoon moments, where Bugs Bunny keeps running and running and the hallway stretches farther and farther.

"What is this place?" I asked as I stepped up next to Eran. Even if it didn't seem like it, we were making our way down the hallway, one step at a time. "Is it heaven? Limbo?"

"Would you like it to be?"

I swallowed. "I don't think so. If it is, it's not what I expected."

"Then it's probably not." Eran's white hair bobbed lightly on top of their head as we walked. "As far as I know, this is just the world. Earth, if you want to be specific. It's an instance of it, one that exists on its own. We call it a moment."

A red door crept closer to us from the end of the hallway. Looking back, I saw myself on the bed, my parents still standing right next to me. Eran and I hadn't moved an inch from that scene, yet the door approached with every step.

When we finally arrived, Eran made sure we stopped a few steps away from the strange red door. Eran held out a hand, stopping me from going closer, still holding their gaze on the door. To me it just looked like a regular, boring old door. It was wooden, painted red at some point, and now flaking and cracking. It had a round, golden doorknob, but other than that, it looked like anyone's old bedroom door.

"I don't know what we'll find on the other side of this door, Jacob. But, all of it will be real,"

"What?" That was odd. "Am I not dead?"

"Things can still be real, even in death. The thing is, we won't be real, you and I. We cannot affect anything we'll see. Can't touch or see or hear. Do you understand?"

I nodded. "But it will be real? It will be . . . happening?"

"Yes. Or it will *have* happened, or it *will* happen. One of the three, I can't say which."

Future, past, or present. I think I understood, and I think Eran saw that I did, too.

They gave a curt nod. "Are you ready, Jacob?"

I didn't think I was. How ready can one be to go through a red door in the afterlife? I'm guessing not very. I nodded all the same.

"Sure, Eran. Let's go."

Afterlife

We were in my house. That's to say, my dad's house. Back home. I recognized it instantly. I'm not sure if I saw our old living room through the doorway, but I certainly stepped right into the middle of it, and when I turned to look back, the red wooden door was gone. Everything seemed perfectly normal until I noticed how *old* everything was.

The living room was the one I remembered and loved, so to speak, but not the same one I'd been in last week. This was my dad's house fifteen or so years ago. A thick blue carpet lay under a weird, coffee marble table. I've never known anyone else who had a marble table, not before or since, but we did. It was super cool and incredibly heavy. It hurt like hell when you ran into it.

A whole section of the living room had been rebuilt since I was young. I smiled as the nostalgia reminded me of how it had looked.

"Do you recognize it?" Eran was of course right there, but I'd forgotten and jumped at their voice.

"Yeah, I . . ." I didn't know what to say. It was so unreal. "Have we traveled in time? You said this was real."

Eran's face looked like they contemplated my question and found difficulty in knowing what to say. "Maybe? But not really. Like I said, these are moments. They're still real, even if they happened a long time ago or haven't happened at all yet. We're the ones who are technically not real."

"Okay, I guess . . . What are we doing here?"

Eran almost smiled, but only with their eyes. "No idea."

"What?"

They gave an almost unnoticeable shrug.

I was beginning to get frustrated with Eran. Whoever or whatever they were, they weren't being very helpful. They were the one who had brought me here after all, to this *moment* in my past. How could they not know why we were here?

"Is this about how I died?" It seemed like a logical thing to ask. After all, dying was the one, most major, life-altering event I had experienced recently. It's probably the most *life-altering* thing anyone ever experiences. Pun very much intended. It seemed only reasonable that that might be the focus of whatever journey we were on.

Before Eran had a chance to respond, a boy came running through a doorway, zooming through the living room.

I jolted. It scared the absolute living shit out of me.

Seriously, I thought I was having a heart attack. That other scene, with my parents and me being dead, had been still. Like one of those hyper-realistic paintings. Naturally, I figured this living room scene would be too. Dead and gone. But here this kid came running right past the two of us.

That's when I noticed.

The kid was me.

"Who's this?" Eran asked, with a smirk that suggested they knew.

"It's me."

Little me was running around with a toy, playing. It looked like a plastic spaceship, not one that I remembered, but clearly one I had enjoyed.

"Why are we here?" I turned to Eran as I asked and kept turning in circles to take in more of the room. There was nothing else that jumped out at me, no other people, no other things. No red door.

I met Eran's gaze. "No idea."

We spoke at the same time, as if we had rehearsed it for years, and it annoyed me to no end that I knew they were going to say that.

Why did I even bother?

I locked my sights on younger me, and in a cold shower of déjà vu, I suddenly remembered what this moment was.

Little me went for the patio door. It was nice to go outside sometimes. My dad grew up on a farm, as did I and my siblings, so we had a huge garden with a massive patio. But there was a storm that day.

As soon as the young me grabbed the handle, the door flew up, almost twisting itself off the frame. Terrified, I bolted back inside the house with my little feet. What should have been a fun, lazy day playing inside the house had become something terrifying.

"I remember this," I told Eran.

I turned toward the front of the house. It all came back to me. I had pleaded, begged, and cried to my parents to let me stay home alone that day. I was probably too young (but it was different back then), and they eventually came around and let me stay. They were just out shopping anyway and would be home soon enough. But right then, I was alone.

Eran turned with me. "What are we looking for?"

"I . . . I don't know." We looked back at the younger me.

He was struggled with the heavy door, trying to pull it shut against the howling wind that kept it open and pushed flat against the wall of the house. Eran and I walked closer. Either of us could have easily reached over, grabbed the door, and pulled it shut, but I believed Eran when they said we wouldn't be able to affect anything.

Little me was struggling, a lot. He hung out on the steps leading to the patio, clutching on to the door handle with all his might, but there was no way in hell he could force the door shut over the power of the wind. He could barely stay upright.

"How old are you, here?"

The question caught me off-guard. I figured Eran would know this. After all, they were my self-proclaimed guide, shouldn't they know?

I cocked my head to the side to gauge my appearance.

"Five? Four? I think I'm in the ballpark, but I'm not sure I can trust my memories."

"What do you mean?'

"Well, it just dawned on me. I have all these scenes in my head, scenarios I know I've been a part of. And I could probably put most of them in order of which came before or after the other. But if you asked me to set up a timeline with specific ages for specific events, I wouldn't have a chance."

I pointed to myself. "It's difficult to recognize myself at this age. I don't remember ever seeing myself like this, because when I was that young, I had a different perspective. I was smaller, physically, and at the same time lacked the understanding of the world that I have now. Sure, I remember having seen pictures of myself looking like that, but I don't remember actually ever looking like that."

Eran stared at me. "So . . . four or five then?"

I couldn't help laughing. "Yeah, four or five, if I had to guess."

The doorbell rang and I instinctively moved toward the front of the house. I knew this was about to happen. I knew I was waiting for something. Weird thing was, even if the doorbell was the same one that had been there the last twenty years, the same sound, the same chime, I recognized it as a younger sound. It was as if it aged alongside me, becoming more mature over the years.

Little me left the patio door to its windy fate, running through the living room and hallway toward the main door.

"Who's the man?" Eran asked.

It took me a few seconds to realize we could see him through the narrow windows next to the front door. I knew who it was. I remembered this story. But the weird thing was, I didn't recognize him. At all.

"He's a neighbor."

I thought about it. *No, that's wrong.* "Or . . . a family friend at least. My parents are out, and he came to see if they were in, if I remember correctly. I refused to go. Wasn't such a big deal back in the day. Anyway, the door blew open, and I remember that I couldn't for the life of me get it shut. This guy" — I pointed to the man. He was much older in my memories — "drops by out of nowhere. Perhaps a bit surprised that I'm here alone, but even more so when I . . ."

The man laughed and headed inside, following the young me closely.

"When I ask him to come shut the door."

Eran and I didn't follow them, but we saw him close the door through the long hallway and parts of the living room before he came back down toward us and left. Younger me went back to playing with his toys, as if nothing ever happened.

"What is this?" I asked Eran.

Eran looked confused as they took a quick glance around. It was like my questions were slowly forcing more and more facial expressions out of them, making them just a tiny bit more human. "You said this was your memory, no?"

"Yeah, of course it is. But why this one? What's so important about this that we had to see it?" I saw the answer on their face, just as soon as the words left my mouth.

"No clue, Jacob. Sorry." Eran sighed lightly, putting their hands in their pockets.

Pockets. It was such a casual, normal thing to do, that for a second, I forgot we were both dead. I didn't even realize they had pants, least of all pockets. I looked down at myself. I was still wearing dark blue jeans and a black t-shirt. It looked like it could be one of my band t-shirts, but I didn't recognize the logo.

No, wait.

I couldn't remember the logo. It was there. I knew I had seen it earlier and remembered it fondly, but now it was . . . diluted. Blurry.

"What do you think?" Eran stared at the ceiling, eyes scanning the architecture.

"About?" I followed their gaze. Nothing I hadn't seen before. I had lived under this roof for years. It was a good roof, but all in all, it was just a ceiling.

"About your memory. Why are we seeing this? What do you think this is?"

I felt like I was being interrogated. Not in a mean cop *where are the children kind of way*, with a light bulb burning my retinas; just in the normal *dude, what's with all the questions* way.

My point, I guess, was that I felt Eran was supposed to have the answers, not be asking the questions. I mean, I was the one who was dead after all, and they were this weird-ass androgynous angel.

"You still there?" Eran was staring. I'd been thinking too long.

"I guess this is my first. Or one of my first. Or the one that I pretend to be my first."

"Memory?"

"Yeah. It probably isn't, but your brain tricks you about what you think you know, right? In my mind, this is one of the first memories I have. A baseline, so to speak. I remember it because I thought it was really cool of my parents to leave me alone. Then I was scared when the door flew up and the winds blew through the house, but I sorted it out by asking our neighbor for help."

Eran started walking just as soon as I said those last words, going back into the living room.

"Why are you wondering?" I asked as I caught up.

"Well, it's your memory. Your moment. I was just looking for some insight."

I'm not sure if they got any insight from what I'd just told them, but I left them to it.

We wandered for a moment, looking at things, observing little me running around playing. The more I took in of the furniture, the photographs on the walls, the dishes on the table, the more the memory came back to me. I didn't realize how much I'd forgotten. Nearly every single thing, every single recollection meant something to me, but I'd forgotten almost all of it in my older days. That's what growing up does to you, I guess. Makes you forget.

"Do you miss it?" Eran stood in the doorway to the small kitchen I had aimlessly wandered into.

"I'm not sure. I don't think so. But it's very nice to see it again. This room doesn't even exist anymore. My dad tore it down, made a hole in this wall, and the kitchen is inside there now." I pointed through the shelves and cabinets.

Eran seemed to nod but didn't look like they cared much. "But the memories of this place, they're good ones?"

I wanted to ask about their line of questioning, because it was weird, but I figured I wouldn't get a proper answer anyway. "Oh, yeah. Most certainly. Everything I remember from this place was great. This was before . . . before Mom and Dad separated. Before Ford and I had to move."

We stood there for a while, each of us staring at our own piece of outdated furniture.

"I think we're here to get to know you," Eran said suddenly. "Both to get to know what you were like . . ." They looked down at little me who came running through the room as if on cue. "But also, what you're like now."

"What do you mean?" Eran was on the move again, and I was eager to follow.

"The events in our lives that become memories change us. You've become who you are because of what has happened to you in the past. It will be good for us to know how and why."

"Why though? Why do we need to know who I became?"

"I couldn't say, Jacob."

Of course you couldn't. I wasn't asking why *they* specifically wanted to know, but they probably knew that. "I already know who I am. I could tell us what we need to know."

"Do you?" Eran stopped to look at me, and for a second something in their gaze made them seem wholly inhuman. "Do you really?"

"Yes!" A frustrating warmth rose within me. That's when I first noticed how familiar Eran was. I couldn't tell you why, but there was something about their bland, featureless characteristics that I recognized.

"I think we're done here," Eran began, shifting their feet to move away, but I wasn't ready.

"No, we're not! I need to—"

Eran pointed past my head, nodding toward something behind me. "I really do think we are."

I turned toward the front door. Except it wasn't the one I grew up with. It wasn't the really heavy brown one I slammed when I was angry or threw open with glee as I came home from school. It was the red door. The one I thought I recognized but couldn't remember where from.

"Shall we?" Eran asked.

Home

e were back in the living room of my dad's house.
What the actual fuck?

We stepped through the red door only to step right into the middle of my childhood home. In total, we traveled about thirty yards. I was just about to ask Eran what had gone wrong when I realized we probably traveled much farther than that, just not in distance.

Most of the furniture looked the same, but some had changed places. As I turned toward the end of the living room to orient myself, I noticed my dad was there. He was standing with his hands on his hips, looking down at a child on the floor.

"Your father?" Eran asked. Something in their voice suggested that they already knew who it was.

"Yeah, that's him." My own voice was careful, almost whispering. I think I was worried I was going to scare him away like a nervous deer. But of course, my dad couldn't see or hear me. He looked so young. So incredibly young.

"Is that you?" Eran nodded toward the kid next to him.

All I could do was smile. "No, that's Ford. My younger brother."

Ford was never a big kid. Not even by the time I died, and he was fifteen by then. But he was particularly tiny as a child. Thin and slender, with blonde locks that draped over his shoulders.

The moment reminded me: I think I knew what was going to happen. I took a few steps back toward the doorway that led from the living room to the kitchen. There I was. With Mom.

"I'm in here," I said to Eran. "We're making dinner. Pizzas. I'm just old enough to make my own." On the kitchen table was a pizza made for Dad and Ford. The front door slammed shut. Hard. "And that would be Nina, coming home for dinner."

I wasn't wrong. My then-younger, older sister came striding through the living room from the side door, pitch-black hair flowing behind her. I wasn't able to move out of the way for her. She walked straight through me.

The sensation sent me to my knees. An icy chill struck every bone in my body followed by what I think was a searing pain. Had I not already been dead, I would have thought that that was it. The feeling was overwhelming. Like an extreme, all-encompassing pins and needles.

"Oh God, what the fuck?" I yelled at Eran.

"Yeah, I forgot about that. Try to avoid people. I don't quite know what causes that, but it can be excruciating."

"Why is there pain in the afterlife?" I wheezed as I struggled to my feet. "I thought everything was unicorns and marshmallow clouds."

"What gave you that idea?" Eran almost smiled, turning

around as if to look for unicorns. "And you've heard of hell, right? There's a whole afterlife department dedicated to pain and suffering."

"Yeah, and this is it?" The pain was still making me tremble, like an electric current going through my body.

"No, of course it's not. But pain is inevitable. Unfortunately, when people inhabiting the moments we visit pass through us, we feel it. Can't be avoided. So, try to avoid them."

"Got it." I stood back up to see my family settling down for dinner in the living room. I loved those pizzas, and I was happy to see my memories of them were correct. We ate, joked, and laughed. I don't think a single one of us even noticed what was on the TV.

"And what's the purpose of this?" I asked.

"I don't know—"

"I *know* you don't know." I turned to look at Eran. "Do you know *why* you don't know? It seems reasonable that a guide through the afterlife would have some inside information about what the hell is going on."

Earn smiled, shrugging carefully. "I don't know, Jacob."

"Of course you don't." I looked back at the scene in front of me. "But all this does is make me sad. I miss this. These moments were amazing. Do I have to relive everything I love?"

"Not to tell you what to think," Eran said, gazing across the room, "but you're quite lucky. You might be the only one of your siblings who gets access to these moments."

I gazed over at Eran. Their still features gave me no sense of, well, anything. "Why?"

"Because they're yours, of course. Sure, you might share parts of them with your siblings, but these are all your private moments. All just for you."

Eran had to have had a life, even if they looked weird. Even if they spent their time guiding me through the afterlife. "Do you miss stuff, Eran?"

"There are many things I miss, Jacob, but this isn't about me. It's about you. Come here for a second."

We stepped to the edge of the kitchen. It felt like we were stepping out of earshot so that my past family wouldn't overhear us, but of course it was only so we wouldn't be bothered by the noise my younger self and siblings were making. Turns out, a ten-year-old is loud.

Eran held out a hand toward my family around the dinner table. "How would you characterize this memory, Jacob?"

"I don't know." I shrugged. Not because I was careless, but because the question was weird. "Good, I guess?"

"So, it's a good memory. Memories — or moments — fall into one of three categories." Eran began counting on their fingers. *One.* "The good ones. Those are the happy, smiling, laughing ones."

Two. "The sad ones. The ones that tear at your heart. Make you cry, makes it hard to swallow, the ones where you break up with a girlfriend or your best friend moves away."

For a moment I thought back to my first girlfriend at age eight. I hadn't felt like that at all, but then again, we were children.

Three. "And the last ones are bad memories. The kind you wish you were without, completely. Not just sadness, but regret, shame, when you did something truly horrible, or experienced something awful."

I tried to think what those could be, and my face must have given it away.

"Most people think they don't have any of those, but everyone does. Something you wish you could take back." Eran stared at me so hard I thought they were waiting for me to confess something.

"All right. And what does this have to do with my purpose?"

"That's it, unfortunately."

"That's . . . that's not helpful at all."

"I'm sorry, Jacob."

I left them behind, going back to my family. It was later in the evening now, somehow. Younger me was already in bed, only my sister was up with our parents.

I guess time flows differently here.

I reached out for my dad's shoulder, not thinking about the consequences as my hand began falling through his body. Stinging barbs of pain erupted in my fingers as soon as it slipped, and I quickly withdrew.

"You can't—"

"I know I can't! Would you just let me mourn for a second?" I stormed out of the living room. It wasn't Eran's fault, but at the same time I just wanted to be left alone.

They found me in my father's office a while later. I don't know how long I'd been there, but I imagined it was quite some time. Eran's struggle to find me was perhaps because the door was closed. It had been when I went up to the office, but of course, that didn't stop me, I just walked straight through it.

"Is this what dead people do? An eternity of reliving the past? Haunting themselves in old memories?"

"They're moments actually—"

"Sorry, yes. Moments. Goddamn moments."

"And no. You don't haunt the past. I'm sorry I don't have all the answers, Jacob. But consider for a moment, that maybe we haven't even found the questions yet. All of this is your life, your memory. Every single moment is something you've lived. In fact, the only reason we are able to go in here is because you've been here before. You know what this looks like in your mind's eye." Eran pointed toward the top of the bookshelves. "See that gray blur?"

I did, and it disturbed me. At the very top of the bookshelf, the world was static. Like on the television. It was flipping in and out of reality.

"That's because you don't know what's there. Or what was there, I suppose. You never looked up there when you were little, so you can't fill in the blanks."

I stared at it for a while longer. "Huh. Weird."

"It is a bit weird, isn't it," Eran said, and for a moment I could swear they smiled. "My point is that you're the one who knows this place. I don't even know what we're looking at, nonetheless what we're looking for. But I'll help you look. As best I can."

Mom was calling me. Instinctively, I was halfway through the door — the actual physical door — before I caught up with the thought that of course she wasn't calling *me*, she was calling younger me.

But I went to bed?

Except, when I came down, it was earlier in the evening again. Younger me came running into Mom's arms, and all I felt was envy. Sure, it was a happy memory, all in all, but I also felt like I was being ignored by my own family. It was heartbreaking. And the worst part was, I didn't even dare go near them, afraid of the debilitating pain I would feel.

I sensed Eran walk up behind me. "Fine. What do I have to do?" I asked.

"The red door. We have to find it. It's the thing that leads between these places."

"And where exactly are we going? To a new memory — sorry, *moment*? Why? When does it end?"

"You're very inquisitive, Jacob." Eran said with warmth that made it sound like a compliment, but I sensed a 'but' coming. "And that's great. But let's save some questions for later, alright. Let's focus on finding the door now."

I had more questions, but I also had all the time in the world. I could probably save them for at least a little while.

We searched the house up and down. At first, in all the places I knew there would be a door (I grew up there, after all, you would think I'd know). But of course, this magical portal to the different moments of my life had a tendency to appear slightly out of place, not bound by the laws and regulations of regular doorways, so after a while, we started looking everywhere else too. We didn't find it.

"We'll find it when we find it," Eran assured me, but that wasn't really reassuring at all. It was infuriating. Were we just supposed to wait around until the door decided to show up?

After running around the house, up and down the stairs for hours, occasionally running into Eran and visions of my past family, I sat down on the stairs — though I'm not actually sure I physically sat on the stairs or just hovered right on top of them.

"Who are you?" I asked when Eran came up to me.

"Eran. You know that."

"Yeah, but . . . who is Eran?"

Eran's head twitched a bit and their gaze unfocused. I think I caught them off-guard.

"That's me. Are you confused, Jacob?"

"No, it's not that. I'm just wondering who you are to me, in a sense. Why are you the one who does this? Do you guide every dead person through the afterlife? Or is it just me? Where do you come from?"

"I don't guide anyone but you, Jacob. It's just me and you. Like I said, I'm no angel."

"Yeah, I'm beginning to understand that."

"That doesn't mean I don't have a few tricks up my sleeve."

They headed up the stairs past me. "Come along now. It's starting."

I turned to see Eran arrive on top of the stairs, then turn right into the bedroom.

My bedroom.

When I entered that old bedroom I had spent so many years in, I found myself and Mom huddled up in the bed, Eran leaning against the window sill. Mom was reading me a bedtime story.

It wasn't one I remembered, which I thought was a strange, but warm nostalgic glee filled me nonetheless. I stepped in, taking a spot in the middle of the room, afraid I was going to disturb their little séance.

By the time my mom finished, I was asleep. She leaned in, kissed me on the forehead, and whispered: "I love you."

The young me heard her say it only barely, because I was about to fall asleep, but I could read her lips. I caught Eran grinning in the corner of my eye.

"What? Did your parents never tell you they loved you?"

"Of course they did. But did you know that yours did?"

He's got me there.

Of course I knew. I knew they cared about me. But Eran had a point. There was something special about seeing it being said to me without my knowledge. It made me sad. Sad that I had to leave this place, sad that I didn't get to experience it that time. I had missed it, and now I had been reminded of that.

"Job well done, I guess." Eran stepped past, pointing behind me. I turned to see the door to the hallway was bright red. "Let's go."

Purpose

We stepped out into a living room side by side. I recognized it after a few seconds of course, but Eran seemed more confused than usual. It's not like they had grown up in my childhood home, but they hadn't looked so shocked there as they did now.

"Mom's apartment. After the divorce, Ford and I moved here to live with her."

"Right. How long did you live here for?"

"A year, I think. Longest year of my life. We rented it until my mom could afford something different. I remember when we moved to the next house, because it fell almost exactly on my birthday."

I took a walk around, reminding myself of how the place looked, and realized no one was home. Mom was at work and my brother and I were at school.

"I don't suppose we can make the red door appear all on our own?" I turned to Eran who looked quizzical. "We have to observe some memory, or moment or whatever, first?" They only nodded. "Guess we're stuck here until someone comes home then."

It wasn't a big apartment. The front door opened up into a hallway, with a bedroom on the right and a bathroom on the left. The hallway led directly to the living room and combined kitchen. Take a right again in the back corner and that was my mom's bedroom.

That was it. That was all of it. Compared to the big farm-house I grew up in, built sometime in the early 20th century, this apartment was super tiny. Took me less than thirty seconds to walk through it all, then I sat on a kitchen chair — that I imagined I was able to sit on, even though I couldn't interact with anything — and waited.

Eran seemed more interested than usual. They walked around, pacing slowly with their hands behind their back taking it all in with deep sighs.

I wanted to ask what they were doing, why they were so interested, but at the same time I really didn't want to talk to them. They were the only company I had on this trip of my life, and for a moment, I was enjoying spending at least some of it in peace. I was dead, after all, and I had no idea how long all of this was going to last. Going through my whole life — the little of it I had lived — would take . . . well, it would take twenty years if we did it by the books. It was nice to have a break from reliving it all.

"I guess there's something I should explain." Eran pulled me out of my thoughts as they took a seat opposite me.

"There is?" I didn't like the sound of that. Not just because of the fact that there seemed to be more rules, but clearly, he had been hiding them from me.

"It's something I've come to understand as I've been doing this. Like I said, there are those three different types of moments: good, sad, and bad. That's just what I call them, feel free to call them something else, but you get the point."

"Yeah? And?"

"And what we're doing here is . . . rewinding them, so to speak. We're going through them, checking that they're all what they're supposed to be."

"What does that even mean? These events are all in the past, how could they be anything else than what they were?"

"Think of it like finalizing your purchase. Before you check out completely, we'll look over your order. See that everything is the way you want it."

I sat up in my chair. It was difficult to understand, but eventually it dawned on me what they were saying.

"I . . . Eran, can I alter my memories? Change the past?"

Eran smiled, for real this time. "Yes. But there's a catch."

I almost didn't hear them. That sounded unbelievable to me. Not only did I get to relive my life, but I could change it as well? Where would I start? I could do anything. Become anything. Even if it meant dying at twenty, I could still be someone, create something better, leave behind a legacy.

"Jacob? There's a catch."

I shook my head to get back to Eran. "What is it?"

"Two things, really." They held up two fingers. "First, you only get to change *one* moment. That doesn't necessarily just mean one thing, but it means that you're limited to changing what was said and done during that moment. Second, you have no control over how that affects the future that comes after it."

I took a minute to think about it. I had been too caught up in the opportunity to change my past, that it was difficult to comprehend what Eran was saying.

"Just one thing?"

"One moment, yes."

"Easy, I'll stop myself from dying."

Eran pursed their lips. "That's not a moment, in the true sense of the word, unfortunately. That's more of an *event*. You can't stop a thing from . . ." They hesitated for a moment. "From falling down."

"But you said I could change what was said and done in a moment. I could take a step to the left. Avoid being crushed to death and change my future. I'd be alive."

"Maybe. But you can't be certain that would be the outcome. Not because you're not allowed, but because it's impossible. No one would know the consequences."

"Who decides this? God?"

"Like I told you, if there is a God, I've never met them."

"So . . . what *could* happen? Give me some for instances."

"I don't know. Anything could happen, I guess. Anything might have happened already. The world you grew up in could be affected by someone else's last-minute change to their life. I'm not being confusing on purpose, Jacob, but there's no way of knowing what might have been or what might be. Even for those of us who travel through the red door."

The butterfly effect. I got it. One small change could have huge consequences. Or it could mean nothing. We weren't just talking about changing aspects of my own life, the repercussions could ripple through to dozens, hundreds of people, maybe more.

"How do you know this? You said you guide no one but me. If you haven't done this before, how do you know this is how it works?"

"This is how it works, Jacob, trust me."

"Do I have to decide now?"

"No, like I said, we get to look through your whole order before checking out. We have time."

I took a moment to breathe, not that I needed to. What part

of my life did I want to alter? Did I want to try and not die? If so, how? Going back to the warehouse and stepping away seemed easy enough, but Eran had said that might not fix anything. Maybe the thing that crushed the life out of me would fall slightly to the side as well. Maybe the whole industrial shelves fall and mangle me, and no matter how much I moved it wouldn't help.

Could I change something about myself? My love for music, perhaps? If it hadn't been for my passion for heavy metal, I might have been more attentive, and I might . . .

But how would I do that? How far back would I have to go, which singular moment in my life defined that part of me? And how would that affect my personality? The rest of my life. What if I became boring and lifeless, and what if I died at twenty all the same.

Thinking about it made my head hurt. Thankfully, that was just around the time half my family and I came barging through the door of the tiny apartment.

Mom was carrying a whole lot of shopping bags, and my brother and I — children that we were — were of course not doing anything to help. We were running around, laughing and yelling, having the time of our lives. For a second, we didn't mind that we weren't living *at home*, we didn't care that we had to live in this small apartment away from Dad.

But when my mom came into the kitchen to put away the groceries, I saw that her face spoke of another reality. She was exhausted, worn out, and she had to wipe her eyes as my brother and I came running over.

"What's for dinner?" we both yelled in unison. Before Mom could answer, Eran came over and interrupted my viewing of the little kitchen event.

"What's today?"

"What?"

"You and your brother, you're both so happy. What's today?"

"I don't know." I thought about it, wondering if this could be something special, but nothing sprang to mind. "I'm guessing it's just a regular day."

"Huh. You both seem so happy. I would've thought maybe you weren't, with all of this."

At first, I didn't understand what Eran was talking about, then I realized they meant everything. The apartment. Our lives. "We were children. I suppose we didn't grasp the gravity of the situation. At least not all the time. Any moment we managed to forget; I think we loved it."

Eran stood up, and I settled my focus on younger me and my brother again. "See the door yet?"

Earn shook their head.

I stood up to follow myself and Ford as we began playing in the living room. I had to agree with Eran, we did look rather happy. In a way, it made me sad. Sad that I didn't remember this exact moment, that I couldn't tell what day this had been. Most of my memories of this place, of the time I lived there, were cast in shadows of anger and sadness, not joy like what I saw before me. For a whole year I had lived there, and it felt like a black pit in my stomach.

I hated this place.

I remember dreading coming home to it. Sometimes I would even be crying when I woke up in it. But here I was, staring at living proof that there had been great times as well. It was as if they had been washed from my mind.

Then my mother called, and the children ran off, leaving me standing behind like the ghost I was. As they settled in to eat and laugh, I felt an urge to check where Eran had wandered off to (not that there were many places they could go), but something in me figured it could wait a little while longer. It was good to see myself be happy like this.

I don't know how long I watched my little family eat. It could have been fifteen minutes or two hours. Time has a funny way of not really existing when you're totally engrossed in a moment . . . or when you're dead. I had noticed back in my childhood home how my experience jumped back and forth between different instances of the same memory, and though I wasn't getting used to it, I was at least aware of it.

Instead of being caught in the flow of time, traveling along a line from A to B like all living creatures, I had the sense of looking down at it from somewhere else.

My brother and I ran to the TV after dinner, leaving my mom behind to clear off the table. Not a big sin among children, but a sinking feeling stuck in my stomach when I realized my mom did the dishes by hand. For some reason, I had never noticed that we didn't have a dishwasher.

A noise tore my attention away from my laboring mother and I swung around to see myself fighting with my brother.

Just then it hit me. It hit me what today was and why I didn't remember the happy, pleasant memories of earlier.

There was yelling. We were calling each other names. My mom left her chores behind and rushed over to put an end to it, but she was too late.

It was all about the remote to the TV. I wanted to watch one thing, Ford something else. Being five years his senior, there was no chance in hell he could win. I was eleven after all, and even if we had been the same age, I was always a much bigger, chunkier child. It ended with me tearing the remote of out his hands and kicking him off the couch in the same movement.

I had won.

Don't do it, Jacob.

I stepped closer, watching the rest of the scene unfold. I was victorious, standing on top of the couch. Mom was yelling. Ford was crying. I was mocking.

Don't do it, Ford.

But he did. Ford stood back up. He yelled at me. I didn't even hear the insult. I don't think I remember quite what he said. But I was angry. So very angry. I threw the remote straight at his face.

This was back in the day, the good olden times before TV remotes were made of the much cheaper and sensible material: plastic. We had a heavy metallic one, the kind of thing that was engineered to survive an impact or two with a collection of facial bones. Coincidentally, in the face of a six-year-old it can do a lot of damage.

I wanted to turn away, too ashamed of what I had just seen myself do, but at the same time, I couldn't. Ford's nose was bleeding profusely. Younger Jacob's face was white as a sheet, slowly realizing the damage that had occurred at his hand. Mom was yelling, of course, but I didn't listen.

"How's it going?" Eran asked from my side.

"I get it," I said. "This is one of those bad memories. One of the ones I wish I could take back."

"Yeah. We all have them."

All I wanted was to apologize. To pick my little brother up and hold him, hug him and tell him I was sorry. But it wouldn't work. He wouldn't feel it, and all it would do was to cause me pain.

"If I wanted, I could change this?"

Eran cocked their head. "Yeah, if you wanted. You could not throw the remote."

It was a possibility. Not the kind of thing I had initially planned on changing, but certainly a valid choice now that I relived it.

"But..."

"But that could result in me just doing something else to him, right? Not throwing the remote doesn't mean I don't punch him instead."

Eran tipped their head with a careful nod.

"You know what the worst part is, Eran?"

The moment flashed forward to Ford being served ice cream by Mom, and Eran was caught up in observing the sticky goodness fall off Ford's spoon.

"I remember that I did this," I explained. "But I don't remember it being like this at all. In my mind we didn't have a great day like this, we didn't run around having fun. It was a terrible day. Ford and I were shouting and fighting constantly, all day. Mom was angry, everyone was angry. And when I threw it at him . . . it was because I was losing an argument, because everything was so unfair. I don't recall being the one who won, and then kicking him to the floor." I sat down by the kitchen table again. "I love Ford. Always have, always will. We were the best of friends, growing up. Sure, we fought, a lot, occasionally, what siblings don't? But this memory — *moment* — makes it look like we didn't. It's all so confusing."

Eran was still caught up with Ford across the room when it struck me.

"Eran?" I raised my voice just enough to make them turn and waved them over. "How do I know that these memories are real? Can they lie? Can I be certain this is how it happened?"

Eran didn't answer right away. Their face curled with a smile that made it look like they found it an amusing possibility. "These are all your memories, Jacob. Only you know if they are true. But I know that we can't see anything you haven't experienced. That's why we can't leave the house. We can't hear anything that's out of your — the young yours

— earshot. In fact, the only reason we can walk into a different room than the one that your young self is in right now, is because in your head you know what it looks like. Everything we see and hear must have been experienced by you when you were younger. So, the answer is no, they can't lie."

I knew it was true as they explained it, but parts of me still didn't want to believe it.

"That being said, memories are complex things. I would be surprised if this is the only one that you find to be different than what you think. As we grow older, we color them. With fantasies, with added excitement or horror, all depending on how we want to perceive them. Or perceive ourselves. This is why I keep underlining that these are *moments*, not just memories."

"Wait, so my memories — these moments — aren't accurate?"

"They are. I'm just saying that how you think they happened — how you remember them, and how they actual took place — might be two slightly different things." They turned to look at my mom and Ford, still enjoying their ice cream. "But this is hardly the first time you've been mean to your younger brother, is it?"

I was taken by surprise. Of course, Eran was right. As an older brother, I spent a fair share of my childhood mocking my younger brother. But the way they said it sounded so accusatory. So judgmental.

"Of course it isn't. I mean, what siblings don't fight? I fought with Nina throughout the years as well. I've beaten up Ford more times than I can remember — nothing too serious of course, but that's how it went. I was the older brother, he the younger. The same thing would happen to me if the cards were reversed. That doesn't mean I don't care for him and love him deeply. He's still my only brother and my only younger sibling."

"I don't doubt that, Jacob." Eran sounded like they might have more on their mind.

It was late now, for some reason. The ice cream was all gone, it was dark outside, and us kids were getting ready for bed. While we — the younger me and my brother — ran around, Eran and I did our best to stay out of the way, not wanting another bout of ethereal pain.

After a while, I followed Mom and little Jacob to bed. I had overheard mom scolding me, and I'm not sure if it was the shame or the guilt, but I wanted to hear it again.

"Why did you do that, Jacob?"

I heard her say it clear as day even though I was standing in the doorway. It was imprinted in my mind. I was wondering what the younger me was about to answer because for some reason I couldn't remember my side of the conversation, but unsurprisingly, I just cried.

"Your brother got hurt, you know. A lot."

Eventually, I spoke up. "He started it," a younger me sulked.

"You're his older brother. Whatever Ford did to start the argument, you could have stopped it."

My younger self produced a grunt in disagreement. I was beginning to understand how I ended up the victim in all of this.

"If you were arguing about what to watch, you should have talked about it." Mother wasn't finished scolding me and took me by the arm. "You love so many of the same things, there's no need to fight."

"It's not fair!" Little Jacob screamed at her.

"What's not fair? It wasn't fair that you threw the remote in your brother's face, that's for sure."

I then remembered the whole conversation, and I had to take a step back. Eran noticed my reaction, but of course their attention only got more focused on the younger me.

"It's not fair that we have to live here! I hate this place, I hate it. Everything is awful, every day, every minute. There's nothing fun to do here. I hate it. I hate you!" Young Jacob pulled away from Mother's grasp and jumped out of bed, running out of the bedroom and through the front door. Young me had only been wearing his pajamas, and in October I knew it wouldn't be warm outside.

Mother didn't follow. She remained seated on my bed, crying. Ford was already asleep in the top bunk, and there didn't seem to be anything that could wake him up.

"Where did you go?" Eran asked, pointing at the front door.

"There's a playground right outside. I'm just hiding there until I get cold enough to sneak back into bed. If I'm remembering correctly, I'm under the slide."

The thought hit me just as I saw it glimmer in Eran's eyes, and we both headed for the door. The playground consisted of a small slide and a wooden structure made to look like a castle, painted in glaring colors. Just like I thought, I was sitting under the slide, hugging my knees, crying about how unfair the world was.

"Whoa. It looks a lot smaller when I'm a six-foot ghost." I turned in circles on the spot, taking in the tiny playground. I had never been back here since we moved out, and I realized I kind of missed it. Mom came out, and for a second I was worried Eran and I had left the door open. But of course, we couldn't have. She slumped down in the wet dirt, under the slide.

"You know," she began as she put an arm around me. "Earlier you didn't seem to hate this place so much. Earlier, when you and Ford were playing, you seemed to have fun."

"So what?"

"So, I need you to be strong, Jacob. I need you to be better, for me. Because maybe you don't like it here, but maybe your brother does. He looks up to you, and he had fun with you today." Mother quickly wiped away a tear in the corner of her eye. "But you kind of ruined that for him. I know you miss your dad; I know you miss living there, and I'm sure Ford does too. But he's trying to make it work. He likes it here, as do I. This is our new little home, for the three of us. And you owe it to your little brother to be nice to him. To take care of him."

Young Jacob sniffled, wiping his nose on the sleeve of his pajamas.

"You said earlier you don't think it's fair that you have to live here, but it's definitely not fair that you treat your brother like that." She held me with both arms now, embracing me under the slide.

"I'm sorry, Mom. I'm so sorry. Do you think Ford will forgive me?"

Mom laughed. "I'm sure he will. If you apologize to him tomorrow, he'll forgive you in a heartbeat! Especially if you ask him to play with you out here."

They both laughed for a moment.

"But Mom?" Young Jacob shivered in the cold October night. "Do you think I can have some ice cream too?"

It was a painful exchange to observe, but when they left to go inside, hand in hand, the knot in my throat eased.

"What do you think?" Eran asked as the door to the little apartment shut us out.

"I don't think I can trust my memories as well as I think." My voice was on the point of breaking. "The past doesn't seem to be all that I thought it was."

A melancholy descended over me again, and I decided to

head back. I wanted to see Mom put me to bed. I wanted to be there for when it all felt okay again.

Eran made no move to follow. "Where are you going, Jacob?" they called after me.

"Back inside. I need to remember more." I was about to reach the stairs that led down to the front door of the basement apartment.

I rounded the top of the railing just as I heard Eran say, "I'm sure your brother forgives you, but I think our time here is up." A heavy ball fell to the pit of my stomach, feeling like it wanted to drag me under as I saw that the apartment door was red. I raced down the steps, screaming (I think), and just as I reached for the handle, Eran caught up with me.

"It won't be your mother's apartment when you open that door. I'm sorry, but we'll have to move on."

"But I need to apologize to Ford!"

"No, you don't, Jacob. You already did that, years ago." They put his hand on mine and pushed the handle down. "Now let's go."

Decisions

We stepped out into a graveyard. For a second it confused and frightened me; then I recognized it. It was my local one, by the church I had been to countless times, a few of which were for funerals. The white church stood on a small hill right beside us, and the first thing I noticed was how calm the weather was.

"What's this, my funeral?" I looked around to find the people or event that we were there for.

"No, you won't remember that, so we can't go there." Eran began pacing among the gravestones. "But this grave oddly enough has your name on it."

Again, I was confused for a moment before I understood. "That's my grandfather's grave. Notice the dates? I was named after him. Don't remember much of him, unfortunately. He died when I was very young."

"Oh." Eran stared at the name carved in the rock. "Well, I'm sure he loved you very much."

"Yeah."

It was weird. I felt like I knew my grandfather, even though I hardly remembered what he looked like. All my knowledge of him was from a few pictures and the stories people told me. "They said he was a good singer."

Eran's gaze was still locked on the stone. "Do you sing, Jacob?"

"Yeah. Or I used to, I guess. Not so much now that I'm dead." I spun in a circle again. "Why are we here? What moment is this? There's no one here."

"I think I know what this is. It's called an intermission. Just a little break before we move on."

I took another look around. "And a graveyard is the place to do that? Couldn't we at least sit on a comfortable couch?"

"You're not tired, are you? You're dead. I find a graveyard quite fitting." Eran tore their gaze away from the stone, pacing down the row of graves. I wasn't asked, but decided to follow.

"All right, I'll bite. Why a break? We didn't ask for this, so who booked it in? What's changed?"

Eran didn't answer for a while. They just studied the pristine granite marbling. Half of the time I wasn't sure if they knew what to say, or if they did, they were taking their sweet time finding the right words.

The pause in the conversation gave me room to think about things. Mostly about who Eran was. They had claimed several times already that they weren't an angel, and I was starting to believe them. And it was obvious they weren't God — no way could they have that much authority — and they denied that too from the get-go, anyway. No, to me it looked more and more like they had been pushed into a position they didn't really know what to do with.

"Are you listening?" Eran suddenly asked.

"No, sorry. Not at all."

"I was saying . . . you've experienced one of each type of moment now. A good, from when you were little; a sad, when you were home with your family; and a bad one, when you hurt your brother. This is how your life is tallied. Not by your good and bad deeds, but how you made yourself feel."

"Okay, so what? I have to be my own judge and jury?" I kicked at the ground and a shudder went through me.

"No one knows your life like you, Jacob. You're the only one who's fit to judge you. That's a privilege, not a chore."

Something in the way they said it — as if they were about to scold me — made me stand up straighter. "So, I choose where to go next? How?"

"I'm not quite sure. But I'm betting it involves a red door."

"Of course. And then I get to change one moment."

"Those are the rules, yeah." Eran smiled a lopsided grin, as if they had handed me the reins and was worried I would take us off course instantly.

I didn't care. I needed to figure out where in my life I wanted to go, but not before knowing how to get there. The red door was what I needed, the portal to my memories. Knowing full well that graveyards didn't commonly come with random doorways, I turned and headed for the church behind me.

Eran was somehow right on my heels, even though I could have sworn they were facing the other way when I started walking.

"Are you dead, Eran?"

"Of course I am. I'm here with you."

"But, I mean, did you die? Like me?"

"Everyone dies, Jacob. It's one of the few truths of life."

I couldn't disagree with that, cocking my head to the side as I stepped into the church.

It was just as I remembered it. There wasn't anyone in it, and I tried deciding what year of my life this iteration of the church was from. I knew it was not from the year I died, because they had done some remodeling in the last few years and that had not been added yet. It had to be from when I was young, but I did not remember my church well enough to say exactly when.

"Why a church?"

"Why not?" Eran set a slow pace and took it all in, rolling their neck as they gazed at the painted ceiling and rose-colored windows. "A house of worship for many, but a house of death as well. As good a place as any to go when you're dead?"

"I suppose." I stopped in the middle of the church. Froze, actually. In a way, I was panicking.

"Something wrong, Jacob?"

If my body had allowed it, I'm sure I would be cold sweating, but being dead and all put the brakes on that. "I don't know. I'm scared."

"Of what?" Eran looked around. I think they figured that I wasn't scared of anything where we were then, but they had that protective aura over them that made them want to check.

"I think I'm scared of going back through my memories. What if they aren't what I thought they were."

"What if they're better?"

I didn't know what to say to that. What if they were? Would it be worth reliving them, just to check? It probably showed on my face that I was contemplating things. Eran decided to break the silence.

"You're already dead, Jacob. Your moments already happened." Eran smiled. "You have nothing to lose." They grabbed me by the shoulders and the sensation of touch, real, human touch, rocked me to my core. I didn't know Eran and I could touch each other. Their hands were so warm, feeling more alive than some hands I had known when I was living.

For a second, I imagined them coming in for a hug, but then they spun me around. "And there's our next destination."

The red door stood right there. I wasn't given an option. Eran still held onto my left shoulder, and reached past me, opening the door. Sunlight poured through the doorway, illuminating the church as the door swung open. Eran placed a firm hand between my shoulder blades and pushed.

School

"Where's this then?" I asked, as Eran stepped through behind me, grabbing me to make sure I didn't fall. I didn't think I was about to fall, or that I was even able to fall while I was dead, but I appreciated it, nonetheless. "Did you get a bit carried away back there, Eran?"

I squinted toward the sunlight, checking my surroundings. We were standing on a large patch of gravel, dust whipping up around us in the burning sun. A few cars lined one side of it.

"My apologies, Jacob, but it was time to move on. We have a lot of life to go through."

"A lot? I barely made it to twenty."

"Life isn't measured in numbers; it's measured in experiences." Eran started toward the red building in front of us. "Now come. School is about to start."

I don't know how they saw it before I did, but they weren't

wrong. It was my old elementary school from way back when, a huge, red building, with lots of disjointed parts and sections that had been added over the years as the school expanded. I never realized how weird it looked. When I was little, it had seemed magnificent.

I sprinted after Eran — as much as ghosts are able to sprint — and again tried to date the architecture like I had done with the church.

I knew that they fixed the western end of the building sometime during my last years there, and it didn't look like that was starting anytime soon, so that narrowed it down a bit. I was thinking about what else I could use as an indicator for the year in question, but just as Eran and I finished rounding the little hill that led to the entrance my question was answered.

There we were, lined up in all our glory. The first graders. I didn't remember any of this. I might have thought that I did, but I knew for a fact that it was mostly from a picture I had seen at home.

My mom, along with the other parents, was taking it right then. Eran and I stepped up and I got the most uncomfortable sense of déjà vu I've ever had. If you've ever seen one of those optical illusions where once you finally get it, the whole thing twists into the right shape in your mind and you get a bit nauseated? It was like that. *Exactly* like that. My mom pressed the button, took the picture, and my insides curled up.

"Yeah, memories do that," Eran said right before I asked what the hell was going on. "It's the realization that you're finally here, when it all falls into place. Don't worry, it will go away."

I could not answer, arms wrapped around my stomach, clutching onto my sides, even though they didn't technically hurt. They felt like they should though. I was glad Eran was there to reassure me.

"You look happy. Did you enjoy school?"

To be clear, I come from a very small town. Countryside, almost exclusively agriculture as far as you could see. I mentioned that I grew up on a farm, right? Well so did everyone else I knew, and there weren't even that many kids around. In my first year of elementary school, there were a total of seven kids. Five boys and two girls, and that's including myself. When I looked up at the row of children, trying to shake off the weird pain-but-not-actual-pain I was feeling, I saw what Eran meant. The other guys, my old friends, looked a bit worried. Scared almost. First days of school can be intimidating, no doubt. But young me, young Jacob, was beaming. Proud as could be with his backpack strapped on tight.

"I do look happy, and yeah, for the most part, I enjoyed it. But I wouldn't have known that then, we hadn't even started yet."

"Good point," Eran said with some hesitation before they laid a hand on my shoulder. They pointed up at the sky. "This is going to feel a bit weird. Just lean into it."

Weird was one way to describe it, but not a very good one. When I looked up to see what Eran was staring at, I noticed the clouds were speeding up. Then everything else followed suit. The weird feeling Eran mentioned was like a roller coaster, but inside my body. Thinking it was best to wait until it was over before asking them what was happening, I understood it just as we stopped. My memory — or moment, according to Eran — was fast-forwarding.

It reminded me of those time-lapse videos of the sun passing over the sky as the day passes. But in addition to the sun, there were children running in and out of the school like little ants, and the seasons started passing, judging by the trees.

"Come," Eran said and pulled me along.

There were so many memories, so many moments piled on top of each other that I hardly had time to think or feel anything at all. Good, bad, sad; I was crying, laughing, and fighting. The fast-forwarding didn't even stop. Instead, Eran and I caught up with it.

"Who's that?" they would ask every single time another child appeared in my vicinity.

"Jason, Mark, Timmy, George, Linda, and Carly." I pointed them out as they ran past, barely able to discern them from the blurry mass of time-accelerated children.

"Jason helped me with my math. I helped him with English. Mark was my best friend. Still is. George died when he was sixteen. Timmy always wanted to fight. Linda moved away; I think she's married now. Carly I haven't spoken to in years."

I didn't wonder why Eran was asking questions, I just pointed and replied. When you wade through a flood of your own memories — ones you can hardly remember — you do your best to recall what they are and what is important. You do not have time for much else.

We got older by the second. Taller, bigger, faster. Mark and I would sit outside together while the other kids played during recess. Timmy and I would fight. I would chase the girls through the library, pretending to try to catch them. Jason and I were friends, but we always drifted toward other people in the classroom. George was helpful, but never focused and tended to take the jokes too far.

Occasionally Eran would ask about the shadows of other kids running past, those from other grades, but even if I could have remembered who they were — which I want to say in most cases I probably could — they didn't appear clear enough to us. They were black shades intermingling with the seven of us.

Then there was Mrs. Brusly. Through every single grade, she was our only teacher. It's weird, I know. Instead of one teacher per grade year, we had one teacher per class, and then they moved with us through the years. I don't know why, but it worked.

So, with the exception of some sick days and a few temps that I couldn't remember (who also appeared as black shades), Mrs. Brusly was there for my entire elementary school experience. If my ghostly apparition would have been able to, I might have shed a tear of joy at the sight of her. I began wondering if I died before her or not, realizing I never knew how old she was when she taught us. But it didn't matter. She was there now, and thanks to my memories, I got to see her one more time.

"What do you think?" Eran asked. As soon as they said it, the memory slowed down, back to a normal speed.

We were in my classroom, doing math by the looks of it. Judging by my clothes and how big we looked, I would guess we were in our last year of elementary school.

"Think of what?"

"Your school years. Did you like them?"

"As much as any kid, I guess." I saw we were leaving our desks now. The bell had rung, and we sprinted for the door. We were dressed up. There was a cake on the teacher's desk.

Must be our last day.

"Or, maybe I liked it a bit better than any kid would."

Eran and I stood in the doorway, watching my classmates run past. Of course, we would go on to the same junior high together. Not much would change from this year to the next. At the same time, all of it would change. We had been a single unit at that tiny school. We were going to be torn apart in a few years. As we all started to gain new friends, our old bonds would stretch and tear.

"Mark struggles more with school." I almost choked up saying it, looking at child-Mark as he passed my ghostly self. "He struggles with a lot of things in the next few years. I wish I could be there for him more."

George ran past, and I had to step away to avoid him giving me a painful shock. "George ends up growing up too fast. I think he's the first of us who drinks a beer or smokes a cigarette, and by the time he's sixteen, he steals a motorcycle and crashes it. I feel like I don't even know him by then, but at the same time, he was one of my best friends."

Eran's head turned after George as he left the classroom and sprinted down the hall.

"Jason and I . . . We end up just growing apart, I guess. It was fun being friends when we were children, but we just go in opposite directions after junior high." I sighed as Jason disappeared and the last boy steps through the doorway. "Timmy keeps being the unruly kid who fights. I was so sick of it. The whole thing backfires after a while."

Eran made a noise I assumed was out of curiosity. "How so?"

"Let's just say, there's a summer where I outgrow him. And pay him back." I stepped back into the classroom. Almost everyone was gone. It was just me and the girls, and after a while, Linda and Carly left, hand in hand.

"You really did like school, didn't you?"

Eran was right, so I didn't answer. Crossing my arms, I leaned back on a desk, watching the younger me as I talked to my teacher. I swear, if I wasn't dead, I would be crying. I couldn't hear what my teacher and I were talking about, because I couldn't remember the conversation, but I remembered the moment. It ended in a hug, and just as I leaned in for it, I heard my young self, clear as day: "Thank you."

It would have been Eran who turned around to see the red door, but I was getting the hang of things now. It was almost as if it appeared just as I turned.

"We're done here," I said. "Onto the next."

Expectations

We ended up back in the church. At least we didn't have to walk up from the graveyard this time, because it was pouring rain outside the stained glass.

"Another intermission?" I asked Eran, checking to see if there were people there to be observed or if it was just us.

"Looks like it. We're back to headquarters."

"Why have we stopped heading from moment to moment? In the beginning we didn't have a choice."

"In the beginning you didn't know what was going on. Trust me, everyone needs a tutorial."

"So that's what it was? Training?"

"Something like that." Eran looked like they were cold, sitting down on a wooden bench with their arms wrapped around themselves. I didn't feel a thing. We were dead after all, how would we? "You're in charge now. You're the one who's deciding where we go."

"Really? Was I the one who decided we would end up at my school?"

"Definitely. You didn't think I took you there, did you? I've never been to your school, Jacob."

"Of course not. But I don't understand how I choose. You just pushed me through the door."

"Yeah, but you're the one who made the door appear. It's all you, Jacob. Whether you like it or not."

"But how? And why?"

"I don't know, Jacob. I'm sorry."

I sat down on the bench opposite the one Eran was sitting on, on the other side of the church. Even if I couldn't feel anything — and didn't exhaust myself— there was something familiarly pleasant in sitting down and taking a break. I figured I needed to select our next destination. Make a new door appear. "Did I choose all the other moments too? Why did I choose the school? I definitely didn't do that deliberately at least."

"I don't know."

I don't know. I mouthed the words along with them. "How do we know when we're finished?"

"With?"

I shrugged. "Everything, I guess. We don't have to go through my whole life verbatim, do we? When do we stop this time travel business, and what happens after?"

"I'll let you know when we're near the end, if I see it. As for what happens after, I'm sorry to say I have absolutely no idea. Sorry, Jacob."

"But there is an end at least, right? At some point? I don't have to do this forever, do I?"

"Of course not! There is a limit to how much of your life we're going to be bothered to watch through."

I laughed. At least I think I did, if that's what it's called when you're a ghost. "Was that a joke, Eran?"

They didn't reply, but hugged themselves tighter, smiling.

"All right. Next round, let's go." I don't know how I did it, but I did. I jumped up, and still staring at Eran, I reached my hand out next to me into nothing. When I closed my fist tight, I was holding a door handle, and when I turned to look there was an old red door there.

"Are you coming?" I wasn't sure if it was just because I wanted to get it all over with or because I was happy to finally be charge of a little part of this, but something made me smile as I said it.

And it looked like Eran wasn't cold anymore.

Back Home

Back home, again. My father's house, the one I grew up in, on the farm. It was dark outside, and the winds were whipping up a storm. I turned to find Eran but saw neither them nor the door behind me. I was all alone.

"Eran?"

I had arrived in the middle of the hallway. I walked farther into the house, through the kitchen, and into the living room. *Where the hell is everyone?* All the lights were off and it was pitch dark. In my current dense-less state, there was nothing I could do to turn the lights back on. My hand just pushed through the wall when I tried to flick the switch. I found it weird that I could sit down in the church but not interact with anything else, and just as I figured I ought to remember to ask Eran about it, I decided I couldn't be bothered. They would have some senseless, *I-don't-make-the-rules* answer, anyway.

I walked around the house. Back through the kitchen, down the hallway, into the guest bathroom, up the stairs. There was no one anywhere. Again, as a way to pass the time, I tried dating the house by looking at how the furniture was arranged and how the walls were painted. I had to be younger than seven in whatever year I was in, because the bathroom was painted a horrible pink color. But that's about as far as I got.

After a while, I decided to try the one door I hadn't been through yet. The front. It wasn't like the young me was in the house anyway, so why should I be? If anything, this felt more like an intermission rather than reliving a memory. Of course, I couldn't grab the handle of the front door either, but nothing stopped me from walking straight through it.

It was as dark and dreary as I thought. The clouds hung low and seemed to wrap up my entire world. I turned around instantly, worried that now I could not get back in through the front door. But my ghostly hand pushed effortlessly through it. *Whew.* I wasn't locked out.

Wandering around the farm, I decided to just take in the sights. One last round, for old times' sake. It wasn't as if the rain or wind was bothering me anyway, and I had plenty of time.

Most of it was dark. The barn, the garage, the greenhouse, the shed. Seeing as there was no one home, I was guessing they would be out working. Where else would my father go?

I wandered for God knows how long. I didn't rush. A lot of things had changed around the farm since I was young, and it was fun to reminisce about when we built the new garage, tore down my grandfather's barn, and when Dad brought home the new, really big tractor. When I came to my grandmother's house, I stopped.

Grandma grew up in the same old farm house I did. It was her father who built it. When my father was in his twenties and preparing to take over the farm, my grandmother and grandfather built a smaller house on the other side of the farm and moved in there, which later on just became known as *my grandmother's house.* She still lived there, even to this day, and an overwhelming sadness came over me when I realized had she outlived her grandson.

I stopped at the kitchen window. It was the one I always stopped by. When I was little, I would struggle to reach up and knock, hoping she was home. Then I would run up the steps to the front door and wait for her to come and open it.

I didn't walk up the stairs this time. I stayed by the window, staring through the scraped up, fuzzy glass. Aged by the knocks of thousands of children's hands, and as my siblings and I grew older, by grown-ups. As I stood there, I relived every single moment of my life through that pane of glass.

I saw myself and my grandmother and all those times I had been there. Every time I had run over after school, every time she helped me with my homework, every story she ever read, every Christmas, every birthday, every time we served me meatballs in thick gravy, and then packed my pockets with cookies for the eight-second walk back home. All of it was there, in that small window. I'm sure I was crying, but I was terrified to reach my hand up to my cheek to check because I was worried the moment would fade. I didn't even dare breathe.

In the beginning, my grandfather was there, walking around the house, holding and hugging her. I didn't even know I had memories of seeing him in that house.

Then I grew older and taller. Grandpa disappeared, and grandma grew older and smaller. More stooped and craned. I noticed that the younger me was there a lot, but as I grew and kept growing older, I noticed that I aged more. Time was stretching further and further between each visit.

I tore myself away. I couldn't bear to watch it anymore. My

grandmother had taught me most of what I knew, helped me through each step of my life, and as I grew older and became busy with friends, school and work, I neglected her more and more. Turning back to peek over my shoulder, the image was gone. The glass was dusty, the house was dark, and there was no constant flow of memories.

It was over.

Walking back to my house, I was glad to see the lights were on. Maybe there would be people home, at last. I took a deep breath and walked through the front door.

"Where have you been?" Eran sounded borderline furious. "I've looked everywhere for you."

"Funny, I was just thinking the same thing. Where the hell were *you*?" I was angry and feeling cheated. "When I arrived, it was dark and there was no one here. I was all alone!"

"The same thing happened to me, except it wasn't dark. I arrived and found your family but not you. What happened? Why didn't you come through the red door with me?"

"I did! You're the one who never showed. It was just dark." I raised my eyebrows. "And then I—"

"You what?"

I thought about it for a second, trying to understand what I had just seen, wondering what had just happened, and then realizing I couldn't. "Don't worry about it, let's just figure out what's going on here."

"The living room." They pointed up the hallway. "You should go see what's happening."

The way they said those last words made me hesitate. I stared at them for a while, trying to grasp some meaning between the lines, something they weren't telling me.

You should go see what's happening.

Looking up the hallway, my mind started churning. I searched for a clue of what this moment might be, what I might be about to experience. Nothing about this night stood out. There were no hints, as far as I could see, nothing I could hear that gave me any clues. The hair on my neck rose.

Eran stayed behind as I began the walk through the hallway. I turned to gaze at them, wondering why, and they gave me a single, barely noticeable nod. Did they know what was going to happen already? I didn't think they could, because as they had specified so many times that these were my memories, not theirs. Half the time they didn't even know where we were. Whatever it was they knew, they were going to leave me to it, and knowing that made my stomach drop.

I came to the end of the hallway, where one door led to the kitchen — and through there again to the living room — and the other led out to the washroom. I didn't hear anyone anywhere, but Eran had told me where to go, so I went.

Walking around as a ghost is weird at the best of times, but now it felt like I was moving in slow motion. Like I was wading through a rushing stream as the current pulled me back. Every step was a struggle. The small kitchen was empty as well. I stepped out into the living room and heard voices around the corner. We were all there. Mom, Dad. Nina, me, and Ford.

I peeked around the edge. Us kids were on the couch. Mom was standing. Dad was sitting. But there was something wrong.

Everyone's outline was fogged over. Hazy. Like the kids at school, the ones I didn't know too well. It had made sense then. Even if my subconscious remembered more than I thought and could recall school days I didn't even remember in the slightest, it couldn't log every single person who was running around, even if it was aware of them being there. But this was my family. I knew these people. Why would they be dull and gray?

"We have something to tell you." My dad's voice rang like a

church bell, loud and distorted. I had to cover my ears. It was the most terrifying sound I'd ever heard.

"It's not your fault." My mom's voice was almost worse. A screech, like metal dragging on metal, piercing through the air. I buckled over, landing on my knees, and for a second it was almost as if the impact of the floor hurt me. But it wasn't a physical pain. It hurt inside of me.

"I got you," Eran whispered, grabbing me by the shoulders while I still covered my ears. "I saw that they were like this when I arrived. I knew it couldn't be good."

"What's happening?" I asked. I think I screamed.

Looking over, Nina and Ford were still blurry outlines. Young Jacob, however, was clear as day. Full high definition, every pixel of him shining toward me. He was so bright I could count the tears on his cheeks.

"We're getting divorced."

I don't know if Mom or Dad spoke the words. They were dragged out so slowly, every syllable ringing for so long that I wasn't even sure that's what I heard. But that was what they had said. I knew it was, because it hurt. It burned, like when people from my memories passed through me. It was the worst feeling I'd ever felt, and now I knew why this moment was blurred and gray.

I had tried to forget.

Whatever else happened, I hadn't paid attention to it. Or rather, I didn't remember it. There were noises — my siblings and I, no doubt — and my parents were gesticulating a lot. But I didn't hear any of it. I had blocked it all out back then, so I couldn't remember it now.

Their fuzzy outlines began moving around. I didn't remember this part, but I could imagine we were shouting. Angry shouting, it looked like. I sat down on the floor, Eran still there by my side. It was still painful. An unbearable kind of freezing pain, rumbling through my body.

"Are you okay?"

I admired Eran for caring, but I didn't reply. I pushed myself back against the far wall, making sure to be out of range should either I or any of my siblings start running around, and I watched.

It is strange to watch a memory you have that you don't remember, but it's even weirder looking at one you don't *want* to remember. These figures that I knew better than any other people in the world were completely alien to me. Twisted, knotted shapes, sparkling like snow on a television. One of the only ways I could tell the difference between them was based on height.

"We can go somewhere else," I think Eran said. They tried pulling me up, but I waved them away. I wanted to see, however much it hurt. I needed to experience this. It had never struck my living self that I did not remember this. I thought all of this was clear in my mind. But as my siblings and I dispersed, as my parents left to sit silently in different rooms, it struck me. I knew what it was I really remembered.

"It's over now, Jacob. Let's find the door."

"It's not. Not yet. There's one last thing I have to see."

It felt as if the whole house was vibrating. When I got up, my feet were so unsteady I worried I wasn't going to make it to where we needed to go.

"Are you sure you—"

"Yes, I'm sure. I remember this whole moment. It's one of my most painful memories. But this" — I waved at the living room — "isn't it. This isn't the part of it that burned itself into my brain. It's the wrong bit."

We headed through the small kitchen toward the living room.

Eran had given up supporting me, though they were still close enough to catch me should I fall. Could I fall though? And could they catch me? I tried not to dwell too much on the physics of being dead. As we got to the end of the hallway, we turned to look up the stairs.

"Whoa." I think we both gasped, but mine was much louder than Eran's. "That . . . that looks longer than the last time we were here, right?"

"Definitely," Eran agreed. "What happened up there?"

The stairs disappeared into a dark cloud of blackness. The top of them wasn't even visible from where we stood. Like a stairway to heaven, except it didn't look like heaven up there.

"It's what we're here for," I said, swallowing.

I started the climb, one step at a time. The wall next to the stairs and the ceiling above the ground floor was distorted to accommodate the ever-rising stairs in a way I couldn't even comprehend. One step became two, then three, and soon we could not see anything at either end. We were hovering in the air with black clouds all around.

"I assume this is related to what your parents told you downstairs?"

"Yeah. It's the worst memory I have of this whole divorce thing. It wasn't what happened down there in the living room that mattered to me. I don't even remember that. It's this that matters."

Just as I said it, the top of the stairs appeared through the darkness. It was still confusingly far away, but at least I could see it.

When we finally arrived on the landing, it was obvious where we needed to go. Everyone in my family had bedrooms up there, and there were doors all around. One for my parents, one for Nina, and one for me and Ford, because my bedroom was through his. Two of the doors appeared as normal, light-brown wooden doors. But Ford's was twice as tall, twice as wide, and bleeding black tar.

"Not to give it all away or anything, but I imagine we have to go through here," Eran leaned in and whispered.

I couldn't help but laugh. I was just getting used to Eran being about as talkative as a dead horse, never being able to answer my questions, and trailing off without even finishing their sentences half the time, and here they were making jokes out of the worst pain in my life.

"You don't say." I reached out for the door. "You know, you really have a knack for this whole afterlife-guide thing. You should consider doing it full-time."

"Oh, I am." Eran gave me a faint smile, signaling that they saw through my sarcasm, and followed me through the door.

For all the horror we had witnessed in the stairs or outside the room, the inside of Ford's room was nothing special. It was just his normal bedroom. Mine was off to the side, through another door. But I knew we weren't going that way. I knew why we had come here.

I turned to face Ford's bed. Eran took a look around, probably confused about what was going on, what we were waiting for.

But I knew.

I remembered this part.

After a little while, a child materialized. I think I saw him running in, past us, and sitting down, but it was as if my mind didn't start capturing video until I saw him sitting there.

It wasn't Ford.

It was me.

Young Jacob.

I never understood why I sat down in my brother's room. I don't remember that decision, but for some reason I did, avoiding my own room entirely.

"This is it?" Eran crossed their arms, watching the young me.

"This is it."

I sat with my back against Ford's bed, knees drawn in toward my chest, with my head sunken between them. I was hulking and crying, more than I remembered. Much more.

"And this is your worst memory ever—"

I cut Eran off when I saw Ford enter. It was about to happen.

"I was around ten when my parents said they were getting divorced. Which means my younger brother was only five years old. I have no idea where Nina was when this happened, but I imagine she ran off to her own bedroom. After the horrible news, that horrible conversation downstairs, this is where I ran, to cry and hide. And since it's his bedroom, it's also where Ford naturally ended up."

Whether Eran understood what I was telling them or not, I wasn't sure, but they were nodding along. Little Ford stepped over, and surprisingly (though not for me) he was not sad. He was smiling. Giggling.

"Can you imagine the pain this whole thing forced upon us? Being split up, being told your parents are leaving each other?" I took a deep breath. It rumbled in my chest.

"Yeah, it must have hurt."

"It did."

Ford walked up to young Jacob.

"But this was the worst of it all," I said, motioning back to the scene in front of us.

My little brother put a hand on my shoulder and leaned in for an awkward side-hug. "Why are you crying?" Ford asked.

I nearly lost it then and there. If I wasn't dead already, I would want to be. "Can you imagine that, Eran? Being inflicted with so much pain, so much heartache from such an early point in your life, and you don't even understand what's happening? That was the worst thing for me, when my little brother hugged me and asked me why I was sad, because he was just too young to understand it himself. They didn't even bother to explain it to him, Eran. Is that fair?"

I didn't realize I was shouting until I heard the echo of my own voice. It was strange, I did not imagine there would be an echo in the afterlife, let alone inside my brother's old bedroom.

"I'm sorry, Jacob."

"Why?" I sat down next to a small chest of drawers. For some reason I felt like I needed it. "Why do you care? It's not like I witnessed something truly awful. It's just a divorce."

"I care because it's my job to care. Why do you think I'm here at all, Jacob? You don't share these moments, this journey, with just anyone. And you can't measure pain. Pain is like a color. Red is still red, no matter the shade. Don't be ashamed that this is awful for you."

There was a pause between us, the image of Ford and younger me frozen in front of us in two brothers' loving embrace.

"Thanks, I guess. For caring. And for being here."

"You're welcome, Jacob."

"I can still hear him say it, you know. 'Why are you crying?' It tears me to pieces. In one sense I envy him because he was too young to understand. At the same time, I felt awful for him."

"It's commendable that you care so much about your brother, but it's you who's having the truly awful moment here, you know that, right?"

I knew, and yet I also didn't know.

The realization rocked me to my very core.

I had never thought of it that way before. It was always Ford who was on my mind when I thought back to this memory — I never stopped to think about myself. Hearing Eran put it like that, made me feel seen. It made me feel sad for myself in a way I hadn't allowed myself. I was too busy protecting Ford, too worried about my little brother to worry about myself. Eran's words lifted a massive weight off my shoulder. One I didn't even realize I was carrying.

It made me get back up. It made me stand to my feet, take a good look at my brother and me where we sat in a strange embrace of tears. I remembered being so sad, so hurt that my parents had done this to me and my brother. At the same time, it was a relief to remember how little he understood. At least one of us was spared the hurt young Jacob felt.

Then I turned, facing the door to my own bedroom and knowing it would be red, I left the entire moment behind.

Need to Know

Stepping back into the church was like finally drawing breath. The whole world opened up and my lungs expanded in sweet, life-giving bliss.

"I need to know, next time," I told Eran.

They stepped out as if they had not just been in their own personal hell, and when I thought about it, I realized that was indeed the case.

"Know what?"

"What kind of moment it will be. The stuff at my school was fine. I didn't mind that. It's fun seeing it once more actually, because even though it's all up here" — I tapped the side of my head — "I didn't remember any of it." I sat down and took a deep breath. "But those gut-wrenching episodes like what we just saw . . . I don't want more of those. Once in my life was more than enough, thank you very much. I've had my fill."

Eran stopped by the stained-glass window, staring out at what I guessed was nothing at all.

"Sorry, Jacob. It doesn't work like that. The doors open and all we can do is walk through them. We don't get to choose whether they're good or bad, or worse. All you do is make them appear, but that's it."

"You said earlier that there's an end to all of this. You also said I'm the one who chooses, that I'm the one who decides where we go. In that case, I choose to stop now. Take me to the Lord or whatever, I'm done."

"You're very hung up on God, Jacob. Are you religious?"

I shook my head with a sigh.

"Didn't think so. And as I keep saying, if one exists, I haven't met them. Stop seeing this as heaven or hell. Maybe that will help. This is all about you. We're just double-checking your records before sending off your final report, so to speak."

"But for how long?" I shouted. "How much of my record has to be checked? When do I get to leave?"

Eran just stared at me, no reaction to my outburst at all.

We sat for a while. Or well, I sat. Eran remained by the window. It started raining, then it stopped, then it started again. I began wondering if this instance of the church — my church from back home, the one I had been baptized in, and the one I knew I would be buried next to — was real. Was this an actual memory? There were no people here, so I guessed not, but maybe I had fashioned this memory out of some actual—

"It's not. Like I've told you, it's a place for intermission. Based on a real place, not an actual memory."

"You can read my thoughts now?" I should probably have been more surprised, but I was too mentally drained to really be upset.

"No. But remember, this is all you. Your life, your moments, your experiences. Your thoughts aren't as private as you think. But I'm not a mind reader, no."

I didn't bother asking. Or argue, for that matter. It seemed whatever I did, Eran had a way (or found a way) to bend the rules. I wished I could have seen the playbook as soon as we started this thing. Maybe this journey would have made more sense to me then.

"How long has it been? Do you know? Since I died, I mean. An hour, a day, a year?"

Eran's head shifted from side to side, following something outside the window, before they turned and headed toward me.

"Not a single moment has passed yet, since your death."

Not the answer I was expecting at all.

"At the same time," Eran continued, "you've been dead for a hundred years. And more. And less. There's no point in measuring time when you're dead. You're not affected by it. Time is the constant churning of decay. Everything withers and dies underneath it. When you're dead, you're off the team. You sit it out, on the bench, and you don't have to worry."

"Huh," was all I could muster. That was weirdly comforting. For this exact reason, I had no idea how long we sat there. Could have been minutes, could have been days. But eventually, it bored me. "Do you want to see more, Eran?" I got up, looking around, and saw that one of the normally brown, double-doors of the church was red.

Eran smiled that small grin I was getting used to seeing on them. "I'd love to."

Back to School

School. Junior high this time. I recognized all of it and nothing at the same time. It was a cold and desolate place, filled with cold and emotionless children on the cusp of becoming something else.

No wonder I hated it so much.

I didn't recall it being so gray. So incredibly dull. But here I was, and it looked like a movie from the '50s. Everything was washed out, bleak, and dying.

"Whoa." Eran gasped. They weren't wrong in doing so. I understood what they thought. I had the same exact reaction the first time I laid my eyes on it. We had gone from the safe embrace of our elementary school and feeling like we were ready to explore, to venture out into the world to learn more, better, cooler things, and then we ended up here. In this gray chunk of sadness.

"Yeah, I know. Let's go see if it's as bad as I thought."

My school lay on top of a hill. Or, hardly a hill, but a small incline at least. You had to walk around the back to actually reach the door. The front was reserved for a big play area and football pitch that no one ever used. The youngest kids (including myself) went up the hill to the left and used an entrance there. As we passed up through the grades on our way toward the high school, we moved to the right side of the building and started to walk up the right side.

At the moment, there was not a single kid in sight. Assuming we were having classes, I headed up the hill and straight through that wooden door that had ingrained itself in my mind.

"This is different from when I went to school," Eran said as we passed through the cold material. We arrived in a room dedicated to shoes, jackets, and the occasional sports bag.

"Really? When exactly did you go to school, if you don't mind me asking?"

"I do mind you asking, Jacob. But it was years ago."

Eran was getting shifty whenever I asked questions about them, I noticed. When we first met, their features were blank and hard, almost unrecognizably human, and though they still were for the most part, I was getting used to the occasional smile or grimace. But whenever I asked about who they had been aside from being my afterlife guide, they froze back to that uncertain, statuesque appearance.

"All right. Well, this is how it was back in my day. Come through here, I'm probably in class."

There was a class in session in the room we walked into, but it wasn't mine. My year was usually divided into three smaller groups, and though I knew which rooms we had been using when I was a student there, I could not possibly remember exactly where I had been at what exact times.

"Ugh, it looks just as horrible as I imagined it. Look at these kids. They all look so bored."

"I'm sure it wasn't that bad. You're just projecting. Which is why everything is in black and white."

"What? Is it actually black and white?" I had been thinking that was just how I remembered it, but now that Eran mentioned it, I saw that it was actually the case. "And I'm doing this?"

"Of course you are. Who else would be? You do everything to this place, Jacob. You're the only one who can. Whatever we see, whatever we experience, it's all you. There's nothing—"

"Okay, okay. Calm down. Let's see if I'm over here in this other room." I pointed to a door on our left, one of the other classrooms I knew we used regularly, but I stopped and turned us back around. "Hang on! If I'm not in here, how come I have this memory. How come I can see all these places, my friends. How come I knew exactly where they are sitting?"

Eran followed my thinking and gazed over them. "If you were in another class, I assume you knew who wasn't in your class?"

"Yeah, but we were three groups. I can't possibly have known which of the two other groups was in here, or where the ones who weren't in my class were if I hadn't talked to them. Let alone where they sat when I wasn't in the room."

"In that case, I imagine this is just what your brain thinks happened, and it's filling in the blanks. You shouldn't worry so much about everything, Jacob. There are no tricks here, yet you are very defensive about everything that's going on. Let's just go find the younger you, shall we? Take it from there."

"Fine."

Whether I was fine or not, I wasn't sure, but I definitely did not need Eran to lecture me. For a moment I wondered why I kept up with them. Sure, they had been there when I awoke or rose or whatever it is your ethereal body does when you die. But did I have to follow them? Did I have to string them along? Could I fire them and ask for a new death guide?

I peeked my head through the door and as I assumed, there was a class in session. Scanning the room quickly, I deduced that this wasn't my class either. This was the second group, the other one that I wasn't a part of.

"Goddammit. This means that I'm either in gym class or I'm somewhere in the basement in one of the spare rooms. But we used loads of those, so we'll have to look through more than a few."

"Fine by me. Let's go." Eran didn't seem bothered at all, as usual.

We strolled through the library. It was much smaller and more sparsely equipped than I remembered. When I was young, this had been a vast room of knowledge, bridging every part of the school that separated the different years of students. Now, in the body of a relative grown-up, Eran and I crossed it in a matter of seconds. It was a hallway full of bookshelves and a few computers, hardly anything more.

Like with my elementary school, I did not go to a large junior high. We were sixty kids in my year (hence the division into three groups of twenty), and the other two years — there was grades 6 - 8 in my junior high — were probably not much bigger. I'm not sure if that's a big school or not. It wasn't to me. About twenty of the kids were my friends back then. Then you had the other forty who were also *around*. And that was it. For years, that was all the people I knew. Which is why it didn't seem like a lot to me. At the same time, it was loads. I had come from an elementary school where we were only a handful of kids. Then the numbers tripled, and for those of us who came from the small rural school, it was a big change. The overwhelming feeling came washing over me again as Eran and I traversed the library.

We came to a set of stairs leading down to the basement. We shuffled down into the depths of my teenage years, Eran following without comment. One thing I missed from being alive was the smell. I had read somewhere that the olfactory sense was the strongest one when it came to triggering memories, and I wished that I could have smelled those hallways again, just to remember if they used to have a smell at all. But it was all coming back to me, and it was perhaps best that I was not overwhelmed.

"Left or right?" Eran asked as we stepped out from the stairwell.

"No idea."

The basement had classrooms everywhere. But no part of it was officially designated to a certain grade. They were all extra rooms that all the grades shared whenever they didn't have enough room in their part of the school. So, though I could guess which rooms my grade would be using upstairs, there was no way of knowing down here.

"We're just going to have to look through them," I said.

We began with the one right in front of us, peeking our heads through the door and coming upon an aging fat man, teaching math to a bunch of kids who looked like they were about to fall asleep.

"These are the eighth graders, I think. Not my grade at least."

I withdrew from the cold metal door.

It's a strange sensation to put your head through a physical thing. Neither of us appeared as the typical see-through Hollywood ghost. We weren't translucent, we weren't floating, we weren't made of marshmallow. Yet, with some mental effort, we could both traverse any material. Unlike when my sister had run through me, which had hurt a lot, there was no pain involved in leaning through a door or wall. But it was cold. Incredibly cold. Chills ran down my back.

"Let's head down this way, I have a feeling."

I had no way of knowing what day we were in. I knew the year, seeing as I knew that my classmates and I were in the seventh grade, but I didn't know the date, nor the memory. Yet, I had a feeling. A bad feeling. We walked down the long hallway, peeking in here and there, and with every room I ruled out, the feeling grew. It swelled like a sickly piece of loaf, rising in the oven.

Even if I was right about which classroom I was in, that did not have to mean that I was right about the memory. If I'd been down there for classes once a week over the course of a year, the chance was one to forty-something that we would be in *that* memory. Yet I knew it was. It had to be. There was nothing more impactful during junior high than *that one*.

We stopped in front of the door at the end of the hall.

"This is it."

"You're in here?" Eran asked, looking back and forth between the door and me.

"Yeah." My voice was hesitant. I didn't want to admit it, but I had to be in there. And that meant I knew what this was. I knew what was coming.

"You all right?"

"Is it possible that we're here for someone else? That I'm not . . . the main attraction, or whatever."

"No. Sorry, Jacob. No chance."

"But what about all these other kids? We've seen all of them clear as day, as if—"

"I explained to you that that's because your brain is filling in the blanks, choosing a truth to rely on."

"Yeah, fine."

"Are you worried about what's going to happen in there?"

"Not worried, necessarily. More ashamed."

Eran looked at me then, conveying an emotion I didn't understand.

Have you ever lied to someone, and for a second it looks like they know you are lying because they already know the truth? I wasn't lying there and then, but Eran looked at me with eyes that said they didn't believe me, for some reason, and it made me feel incredibly small. More ashamed, somehow, than I already was.

"Let's just go in."

Reflexively, I reached for the door handle, but my hand glided straight through it, followed by the rest of my body. We were in the school's basement workshop. Spread out on woodworking benches were myself and the original six classmates from elementary school, along with a few new faces. We were wearing thick leather gloves and protective plastic glasses way too big for our heads. I stood in the back by a row of empty benches.

"Might as well come here, Eran. The show's about to start." They came over, not exactly hesitantly, but it was obvious they would have preferred to walk around. "You've seen me, right?" I pointed. "Teenage Jacob. On the border of figuring out the world and everything."

"Yeah, I saw. Did you like this part of your life? Do you miss it?"

"Not even one bit."

The teacher had some encouraging words at the end of the class and told us all how great we were and how important it was to be able to handle power tools in the real world.

Yeah, right.

We had made some bullshit wooden sculptures that didn't

look like anything, and we were being congratulated as if we had done something meaningful.

The flock of kids began dispersing, some heading back the way Eran and I had come and some going out the other end, straight out into the courtyard. Young me and the regular crowd from elementary school were hanging back, talking and laughing. This was still just our first year in junior high, and our first year in a new school. We were used to being a small gang, and though I'm sure we had all made new friends already, we were also naturally drawn back together.

All of us.

George, Mark, Timmy, and Linda. Jason and Carly had disappeared with the others. We were all different by then, but to my eyes, I had changed the most. Everyone else still looked like themselves, but my face had filled out different. I had longer hair, and I was taller and broader. George was definitely the tallest. He had shot straight up like a tree. Mark's jawline was setting in, in that particular way that would have girls throw themselves after him for years (I knew only because I'd seen it happen many, many times.) Timmy was his same annoying self; there was just more of him now. He started cutting his hair short, like an army buzz cut. Linda and Carly were grown up too, in that emotionally mature way girls tend to grow up faster than boys.

"Look. It's going to happen any minute now," I told Eran. In one sense I would prefer to leave, or at least look away. But I could not take my eyes off the scene in front of me. I didn't want to see it, didn't want to experience it again. Once had been enough, but I knew how this whole thing worked. To get out of here, I had to go through this.

It started as a joke. Young Jacob liked being the center of attention, especially if he could make people laugh.

We were being boys, rough-housing, and I pretended to

push George, pretended I was going to wrestle him into the ground. Not that there was any chance I could take on George, he was already huge by then, muscular and fit like you wouldn't believe. And that was kind of the joke.

Yet Timmy didn't see the start of the joke. Timmy, who had always been partial to fighting, who started trouble as if it provided him with his life's energy, jumped on my back. It was fun for a few seconds. I remembered and could see on my own face that I laughed. But when he set the chokehold, it wasn't funny anymore.

Snaking his right arm around my neck, he pulled it back with his left hand, and Timmy wasn't joking. He used all his might. I let go of George instantly, toppling backward, trying to pry Timmy's arm off me.

"Jeez," Eran sighed.

My face was going red, purple, blue. When I realized there was no way of getting his arm away from me, I did the next best thing. Timmy had taken to using glasses in his teenage years. He hated them, but he needed them for school — not that he made any effort —and he had put them on after taking his safety goggles off. To free myself from his grasp, I lurched forward as hard as I could, then, when I had gained some wiggle room, I sent the back of my head flying into his nose as hard as I could.

"Holy shit!" I heard George yell from the sideline as I slumped to the floor, free from Timmy's grasp.

Young Jacob would have screamed as well, but I was too busy gasping for air. Timmy was clasping his bleeding nose with both hands. It probably wasn't broken, but blood was dripping profusely, and his glasses had cracked. Timmy shouted at me, George shouted at Timmy, and I was on the floor.

"Were you worried about this?" Eran asked. "You acted in self-defense, clearly."

I held a finger up. "Just wait."

Eventually, Mark joined in on the screaming, and it became a massive fight between the three of them. I was still trying to catch my breath. George was yelling because Timmy took it too far as usual. Timmy yelled that they blocked him out from the fun, always laughing and joking but never including him.

"Three, two, one," I counted, and then teenage me rose from the floor, turned around toward the crowd of three, stepped up in between George and Mark, and punched Timmy square in the face.

"Oh God, Jacob!" Eran gasped.

"Yeah, that's not the worst," I whispered, just as the young me began talking.

"There's a reason nobody likes you anymore!" Young Jacob yelled the words so loud they rang on forever, a constant echo that never ceased. Timmy fell backward on the concrete floor, his skull smacking hard against it. His body curled up like a shrimp, and his hands shot up to his face to protect his ever-bleeding nose.

Then I did it. I arched my back and launched a kick, straight to his core.

Seeing it all happen again made me feel worthless. It had made me feel bad *then*, and came with repercussions that affected both Timmy and me, our teachers, our parents, and our friends, but seeing it again now — from the outside — made me feel even worse, if that was possible.

Young me turned and left, leaving the three of them standing there, George and Mark eventually tending to Timmy. As I left through the door to the hallway, I saw it had turned red. Just as expected.

"Told you so." I looked at Eran and a nervous laugh

escaped me. "I knew we were here for this. My first display of violence. The day I became a bully to stand up against another bully. I'm not going to say Timmy didn't deserve it. Because he was an asshole more than half of the time, and I was so relieved when I finally outgrew him and managed to fight back. At the same time, I knew it was overkill. I knew it was too much."

"You want to tell me why this exact memory has popped into our itinerary?" Eran stood next to a woodworking bench.

"I'd rather not talk about it."

"We have to talk about it, Jacob. If it's supposed to have any value."

I walked around the bench toward the door. "Who knows. Who knows why any of this happens? You said I control the memories we visit?"

"Moments," Eran corrected me.

"Moments, whatever. But I didn't choose this."

"Yes, you did."

"No, I didn't! I don't want to see this; I don't want to experience this again. This is awful. I want to take it back, not see it again from the outside."

"Good. Now we're talking about it."

"Well, I've had enough *talking about it*." I grabbed the handle of the red door.

It was stuck.

I pulled with all my supernatural might, but it didn't budge in the slightest.

"I think we have to talk just a bit longer," Eran said.

"Why?" I turned to Eran. "It's already done. What good will come of discussing it? I'm a bully too, now. Just as good as him."

"So this moment changed you?"

"Of course it did! Don't they all?"

Eran smiled then, wide and proper.

"What?" I still held onto the door handle, and felt it vibrate in my grasp. I turned back toward the door and pulled. It opened and I saw the church shining through from the other side. A warm anger rose in my chest, and I didn't bother waiting for Eran to join me. For the first time since I died, I slammed a door behind me.

Where are You, Jacob?

I used the fact that I had arrived in the church alone to my advantage and headed behind the altar. There was supposed to be a door back there, but it struck me as I went looking for it that I wasn't dependent on a door. It was not like I was going to use it anyway. I would just walk straight through it. I could have just walked straight through a wall. But out of habit, I headed through the door anyway and entered a small hallway and eventually found myself outside the church.

"Jacob?" I heard Eran's low voice call from inside.

Fuck them.

I didn't want to hang out with Eran. I needed to clear my head. It wasn't just about beating up Timmy. It was more than that. I felt . . . shame. Seeing myself from the outside, seeing how differently I had acted compared to how I remembered it made me feel sick to my stomach. In my mind, I had defended myself. I had stood up to a bully. The part where I turned around and punched him didn't seem all that much like self-defense, and the reality of what I had done was hard to swallow.

I didn't like that my memories kept surprising me like this. First with how I fought with my brother, now with how I beat down Timmy. I needed to be alone.

Heading out to the road, I had two options. Left or right. Mom or Dad. They lived in opposite ends of town since the divorce, and it just struck me now how weird it was that the church was almost in the middle. If Eran had told me they had planned for all of this just so this could be the case when I was dead, I might have believed him.

"Jacob, where are you?"

I turned back towards the church, but I couldn't see them, even though the shouting was getting louder. Left or right. Mom or Dad.

"Jacob?"

The shouting was closer. I took a right. Not necessarily because that was my dad's house, but because it was where I grew up. I wanted to see my childhood home.

The way from the church to the farm was a long stretch of straight road until an intersection sent the road flying in lots of directions. From there, a dirt road led past a few smaller farms until you came to ours at the end. Shouldn't take me long to get there, but then again, I had all the time in the world.

"Jacob?"

I heard Eran calling me again, and I jumped because it sounded like they were right behind me. I turned to look, thinking they had caught up with me, but I couldn't see him anywhere. The church rose up behind the trees in the distances behind me, its white spire like a glowing beacon in my land of death.

I wasn't going back.

So far, Eran had been setting all the rules. Giving me things to watch, telling me how my *moments* worked and that I had to pay attention. But had he ever tried to not do those things? If he was a person that died, like me — not that he looked like one with his porcelain grimace and robotic composure — why wasn't he more curious about the afterlife? Why didn't he challenge anything?

"Jacob!"

The shouting was louder, angrier now, and it sounded like it was right next to my ear. I couldn't help flinching, turning in a wide circle to see where they were. They had to be close. But they weren't. Or they were invisible. Either way, I couldn't see them.

I became aware that I could not, in fact, see anything. There were no people walking past me, no cyclists, no cars despite the stretch of road alongside the church being a busy one. Was I in a memory of this particular road? Was I manifesting a specific instance of when I had cycled or walked past there before? Or was this a static image where nothing ever happened, like the church?

The more I kept thinking about it, the more I realized it didn't matter. As long as I got some time away from Eran, from that church and my terrible memories, I didn't care. I'd come halfway toward the intersection now. I was nearly home anyway.

The thing about being in an afterlife dimension is that nothing behaves as it should. Eran and I had already covered this several times, but as I walked for another twenty minutes (at least!) and still found myself in the middle of the church and the intersection, I knew something was up.

"Goddammit!" The distance to the intersection and church on either end seemed to stretch the more I walked. Like when I first rose from the dead and met Eran.

"What are you doing, Jacob?" Eran wasn't shouting

anymore, their voice was calm. Eran still wasn't anywhere to be seen, but if I could hear them, I imagined they could hear me.

"I'm leaving."

"Leaving what, exactly?" their voice said.

"You. And the church."

"Why?"

"Why the hell not?" I grumbled.

"That's not an argument, Jacob."

"Maybe I just wanted some fresh air. Why the hell do you care? You keep saying I'm in charge, that I get to choose. Well, I choose to go home. I'm sick of the red door, sick of watching through my *moments*. It's my fault, all of this. My own stupidity caused me to end up here." I thought back to listening to Iron Maiden and then everything turning black as I died. "I should be allowed to take a break."

"First of all, fair enough. You can take all the time you want. But there's no escaping what you have to do here. What we *must* do. We're on the clock, so to speak."

"Are you doing this?" I spoke louder now, up into the clouds, because that was where I imagined their voice was coming from.

"I'm not doing anything. Like I've told you several times already, this is your world. Your domain. I have no power over you, your memories, or how you choose to experience them."

"Then why can't I leave this stretch of road?"

"Maybe you don't want to?"

"Yes, I fucking do!" Just as I said it, I was catapulted to the end of the road. The stretch before me came flying back like a rubber band that was finally released and I stood at the beginning of the dirt road. I wanted to hurl, but at the same time I was dead and had nothing to throw up.

"Then by all means, go do what you want to do."

"Where are you?" I spoke into the air. It sounded like Eran was somewhere to the left of me, and for a second, I worried they might actually be invisible.

"I'm in the church. Where I'm supposed to be. I'll wait here for when you're ready to go to your next moment."

"Are you not curious what lies beyond that little wooden building? Those four white walls."

"Immensely. At the same time, things change when you die. There will be time for everything later. Going around exploring your reality with you becomes a small drop in the whole of it all. Though I do hope you enjoy it."

"Fine. I shall let you know when I'm done then."

"Good luck, Jacob. I hope you find what you're looking for. When you do, let me know, so we can carry on with the rest of your life."

"What if I don't want to look at any more memories?"

"You have to. It's the one thing you don't have a choice about. You can wait as long as you want, if that's your wish, and I'm guessing theoretically you could postpone it for eternity. But I wish you wouldn't. I enjoy your company, Jacob, but it would mean I'd be stuck here with you."

I hesitated for a moment, in front of the dirt road, listening to Eran. There had been a humming sound when they spoke. When it suddenly disappeared and they grew quiet, it felt like they hung up.

They were going to leave me to it. *Good.*

I started down the dirt road, and realized I had to be in my past. A few years ago (before I died), a big company making parts for the oil industry had bought up most of the land leading to our farm and built a massive factory. As a result, they had redone the road.

But this was the old road, the one I used to walk on to and from school when I was little. There was no ugly, smoky factory in sight. Trees and hedges lined the small road and getting to walk it one more time was a gift I never knew I wished for.

I walked up past the first few neighbors. A house on either side of the road. I had never known any of the people who lived there, and though my parents surely knew them, I couldn't remember ever even asking who they were.

The road turned, leading down a long stretch where there were no hedges, just old stone fences. I had cycled past them more times than I could count, yet now it felt like I'd never seen them before. I wished I could feel the wind in my hair, or the cold, just one more time, but I felt nothing. Being dead will do that to you.

The last farm before ours was our true neighbor. The one I knew. He had not run the farm himself for as long as I had lived, instead, we rented his barn and fields. He was hilarious, always quick with a joke. I tried remembering the last time I saw him, probably at my dad's house, but it must have been years ago. After a small bridge that crossed a shallow river, I was on the last stretch of road leading to our farm. I was going home.

"Is it everything you hoped?"

I jumped. I think I screamed. You would think being a ghost would make you immune to other ghosts, but I've never been more frightened in my life (or death).

"Jesus Christ, Eran! Don't ever do that again."

"Sorry. Didn't mean to scare you."

"What are you even doing here?" I stopped in my tracks, just outside the stone fences that officially bordered my homestead. Eran was a step ahead but had stopped to look at me.

"You triggered a moment. I came to watch it with you."

"What? No, I didn't. I didn't go through a red door or

anything. I'm just wandering, I left the church, and—" I turned to point, and my words caught in my throat.

A child was heading right for me. On a little red bicycle. I barely jumped out of the way before he cycled right past me.

"I beg to differ," Eran said with a smile, wider than usual. Then they carried on after the child. After me. On my red bike.

I caught up as we entered the yard, stealing a shortcut through the garden toward my old house. "What's the deal? I don't get a break?"

"What do you want a break from? You're dead, Jacob." Eran seemed determined, walking straight toward the house.

I got a glimpse of my younger self in the garage, putting the bike away. I stopped and watched. I could not be more than six, seven at most. An unsettling rumbling in the pit of my stomach had me worried about what kind of memory this one would be. Nothing at the top of my head struck me as a vital part of my life at this stage, but then again, I didn't remember even half as much as I thought I did.

"I was enjoying a nice walk down memory lane, thinking I didn't have to worry about being on display."

Eran turned, an annoyed grimace on their face. "All of this is memory lane for you. It's the whole point. I'm sorry if it's difficult, but it's the rules." They swung back toward the house.

"Whose rules?"

Eran spun around again. The annoyance had morphed to frustration. "I don't know, Jacob."

"Then why the hell are we abiding by them?"

"Because we must!" That shout was the largest display of emotion I had seen from them. It was like everything else, combined, times ten. Eran closed their eyes for a second and took a breath. "I'm sorry. I didn't mean to yell. Sometimes we have to do things we don't like, Jacob, for reasons we don't understand. Thousands, millions, of people follow rules they don't understand every single day. Just because we don't agree with them, doesn't mean they don't apply to us. I don't know who makes the rules, Jacob, I just know that we have to follow them."

I sighed. I wanted to get angry, but it felt hopeless instead. "Fine. What happens when we're done then? Do you know anything about that?" I ran ahead of them, standing on top of the stairs to the front door, looking down. "Where do I go?"

"I don't know." Eran smiled, but I think they only did it to disguise a sigh. "I'm sorry, but I don't know."

I stopped to look at them. They looked strange, for a moment. They *were* strange, of course. Pale and without many, if *any*, defining characteristics, but it felt almost like I was meeting them for the first time all over again. "Where do *you* go?" I asked.

"What do you mean?"

"When we're done here. This is all about me, which you've pointed out so many times, even though we don't know why I'm doing this or what happens after. But what about you? Have you done this before? Have you ever seen it through to the end? Do you get a new dead kid to take under your wing when I'm gone, or what?"

Eran smiled with a little shake of their head.

"You don't know, do you?"

"I haven't done this before, Jacob. And no, I don't know anything about what comes after."

Eran didn't seem so alien to me anymore. I smiled back at. "Alright."

I turned back around just as young Jacob came running up the door, and I wasn't quick enough to get out of the way. He grazed my arm as he went inside. It burned like a searing-hot poker. A stinging, both warm and cold at the same time.

I jerked my arm and cradled it in my other hand. "Dammit! Why does it hurt so much?" I grumbled. The pain continued to sizzle beneath my skin.

"The past hurts sometimes. Let's head inside." Eran indicated with their hand toward the door and I gave in, walking through.

We found me in the kitchen, doing homework. No one else seemed to be in yet, and I could imagine my mom was out with Ford and Nina was in school or at soccer practice. Dad would be somewhere outside, tending the farm.

"Were you always this good?" Eran asked.

"What do you care?" I knew what they meant, looking at Jacob doing his homework straight home from school, no muss, no fuss.

"I care very much about you, Jacob."

Sure, I thought to myself and shrugged. It was their job to care. "Yeah, I was usually happy to do my homework. When it was difficult, I'd go ask grandma for help. Most of the time however, I was happy to get it out of the way as quickly as possible."

I took a walk around the house. The living room, the bathroom, upstairs. Everywhere was empty, but I didn't really care. I was just happy to have the house to myself one last time, to walk around and see how much things had changed since I had grown up.

It's not really a thing you think about until you see pictures of when you were younger, but a home can change a lot over the years. You move the furniture around, take down some photos and hang up some new ones. My dad had taken down more than a few walls and remodeled since I was a child, and I had almost forgotten about all of it.

"This is it," I whispered to myself as I stepped into my old bedroom. My favorite bed, just the way I remembered it. I don't know why I said it, but I had a feeling I wasn't going to want to come back — unless some stupid memory forced me.

In one sense, it felt like moving out. Just . . . on a more permanent basis. One last look through the whole place before I shut off the lights, closed the door, and locked it up for good. My finger glided straight through the light switch before I remembered I couldn't touch it.

It was good while it lasted, I thought to myself. *This was a good home.* I came back down to find both Eran and the younger me gone.

"Eran?" Just as I spoke, I knew they wouldn't be around. His tendency was to cling to my every move, or they would be gone for a while. *Whatever.* I would find them when I found them. I was more interested in where young Jacob was. Everything else had been significant events. Everything else had been a memory that, while hazy or partially forgotten, ended up being something momentous in my life. This had to be something similar.

I had not gone through a red door this time, and there was nothing here that reminded me of anything. Nothing I could find made this day special.

Seeing as it had been a particularly beautiful day, I figured maybe I had gone outside to play, so I stepped through the door. Walking leisurely around the house proved what I had thought about the weather, but I couldn't find myself anywhere.

"Eran, where are you?" I stopped as I called for them, hoping their voice would appear inside my head with some wise-ass words of wisdom.

Nothing.

Mom's car was gone, probably out and about somewhere with my younger brother, but Dad should be home. I guessed he would be in the barn. It wasn't unusual that I took an opportunity or two to join him in there, to run around and play with the pigs.

Stepping inside a pig house is a revolting experience according to many of my friends. I had never been bothered. I obviously grew up with the smell, and though I could hear and see in my state of deadness, I could not smell a thing. I wished the afterlife would have implemented some more smells in their memory services. Just one last sniff, for old times' sake. It would have made the memory complete.

No disgusting scent of manure, no air thick with dust filling my lungs. Even the sounds were only partially there. The squealing and howling of pigs echoed somewhere in the back of my mind, but it was muffled. I walked through all three of my dad's pig houses without finding either him or myself. I saw blurry silhouettes of pigs and piglets, and for a second, they looked terrifying. Realizing that I could attribute the haze to my memories not being able to lock on to one single pig-event helped, but they still looked freaky. I had seen so many of them so many times, why could they not appear as the weirdly beautiful creatures they were?

Whenever my dad constructed new buildings, he built them all so that they connected to each other, either by being wall-to-wall or through a walkway. So, after I had walked through all of them, I was at the other end of the farm. I came walking back toward our house from the other end. That's when I saw him.

Me.

I was in the garden on the opposite side of my grandmother's house, the one that faced our neighbors. No wonder I could not find myself, I hardly remembered ever going there in the first place, but there I was, playing in the grass with my favorite plastic tractor. It was the exact model Dad drove, just several times smaller.

"What's this then?" I asked myself as I sat down in the grass.

It's a strange sensation to sit down and babysit yourself. I was never good with kids. Mostly, I was awkward, because I never knew how to speak to them. And here I sat talking to my six-year-old self. Luckily, he didn't talk back.

I looked happy back then, and it warmed me somewhere deep inside. A reassuring feeling filled me, that said: *Sure, you're dead, but you did all right.*

Then I heard the scream. Young Jacob noticed it too and turned toward my grandmother's house. It was heart-wrenching sound. I had forgotten the moment completely, but it all came rushing back to me like a searing pain as soon as the noise reached my ears.

My grandmother's house was only one story. A low patio lined the whole side of the house that faced the garden young Jacob and I were in, and a wide glass sliding door led into the house.

I stood up to look for the source of the scream, and young Jacob did the same, dropping the tractor onto the grass. We both froze.

I saw my grandmother come running into the living room. She was so young; I had almost forgotten she was not always an old woman. I didn't notice until she leaned down that my grandfather was lying on the floor.

Grandpa.

I never even knew that I had experienced this, and staring down at my younger self I didn't think I ever realized what I had seen. I had been standing there, watching my grandpa die, right in front of me.

A coldness wrapped itself around me, and darkness crept over us, drowning out the sky. Young Jacob wrapped his arms around himself, still not knowing what was going on, but knowing it scared him.

As I walked back to my parents' house, the world sped up. Several hours had passed by the time I stepped through the front door and found my whole family sitting in the kitchen.

Mom was crying.

Dad was not, oddly enough, even though it was his father who had just passed away mere hours ago. He was trying to explain Grandpa's death to a confused Young Jacob. Nina understood of course, being ten or eleven, and she hid under our mother's embrace, trying to cover up her tears.

"Your grandfather is dead."

I would probably have jumped if I wasn't too shocked by the whole thing.

"I told you not to do that," I said.

"Sorry." Eran stood in the doorway, looking like they were afraid to bother us.

"I don't remember a single part of being out there. I remember this — barely: Sitting there, trying to wrap my head around what had happened, and everyone being sad. I remember hearing my grandma scream. But I don't remember that I saw it. How can that be?"

"Because your brain wants to protect you. Shield you from pain and heartache, and help you survive. Some things get filed away. Especially when you're that young."

"But still, not even a single memory? Not even a fragment? And my parents never told me!" I gestured to them where they sat right in front of me but lowered my hands quickly. I didn't mean to blame them.

"Parents file away things too, Jacob. Your father lost his father, your mother her father-in-law. It must have been devastating for them — and they probably felt like they needed to be strong for you and your siblings . . . and each other."

"I just . . ." I didn't know what I wanted to say, what I wanted to get out. I felt robbed. I remembered glimpses of my grandfather, but hardly even that. Come to think of it, I thought he had died when I was much younger, not when I was six. It turns out I saw the whole thing.

I overheard my parents say he died of a heart attack,. They said it way back when, and then I'd only heard it, but didn't understand. When I heard it now, I heard it all, clear as day. Grandma had been in the shower. No one could be blamed. It was just his age. By the time she found him he was already gone.

"I want to go back!" I yelled at Eran. When I was standing in that garden, all I had been looking at was myself, playing. I wanted to go back and turn toward the glass.

"That's not how it works, Jacob."

"I need to see if he was lying there! I need to know if he was . . . if I . . ." At first, I didn't realize what was happening, but then I understood. I was crying. It doesn't feel the same when you're dead. When you're alive it feels like your head is exploding and it hurts so much. When you're dead it's just water leaking out of your head, and an immense overflow of sadness. And that's worse because it doesn't feel real. I saw the door change the same time Eran did, and I backed away from it.

"No! I don't want to go yet. I want to know exactly what happened. Why can't we go back?"

"Because you've already seen this memory. Twice now, technically."

"What if he was lying there, watching me?"

"What if he was?"

"What if I could have saved him!"

Eran cocked their head, and for a moment I saw that weird, un-humanoid thing in their appearance that I'd seen when we first met. "You'll drive yourself crazy with 'what ifs.' It's time to go.' Eran walked over to the door and opened it. It was the one thing we could touch, the one thing we could interact with. The empty church glared at us, wanting to pull me away from the warm, though sad embrace of my family. I didn't want to leave.

I did not care how awful this memory made me feel, something made me want to stay in it. It was as if I had been robbed of this moment my entire life, and now I felt like I had to make up for lost time. I . . . I owed it to my grandpa to remember him more.

"Come, Jacob." Eran tilted their head toward the door. "It's alright. No one needs you to stay here, you don't have to relive it all again. Twice is enough."

I didn't want to admit it, but I felt relieved to hear them say that. Before I left, I caught one last glimpse of myself, and saw that although I had not understood everything that was going on, I did shed a tear for my dead grandpa.

Death

We stepped through the doorway, but something went wrong. We were thrown around, and I hate to sound stereotypical, but it felt exactly like how one of those bad CGI time-travel warps from old sci-fi movies looks. A tunnel of whirling blue light stretched in every direction, and then we landed on a sidewalk. Had I been alive, I imagine I'd feel it in my feet and knees, but we were fine.

"What the hell is this? Where's the church?"

The place seemed familiar: a row of houses on either side, stretching up and down the street. Though it was a place I had been before, it was not one I could say I remembered.

Eran tilted their head back, gazing up at the sky, closed their eyes and took a deep breath through their nose. "Feel that?" they asked.

"No. What?" I tried to remember where I was. Many of the houses looked familiar, most of them white or light-blue, but none of them stuck out to me. I saw a street sign down the road, next to an old tree, but I could not read it from where we were standing.

"Air. Fresh air."

I took a breath too, and they were right. Ice-cold air filled my lungs in a way that made me feel almost alive. Then I felt and knew what they meant. Wind. It caught my hair, making it tickle down my neck. Air. I could finally smell the air.

"What is this place? Why can I feel the wind?"

"You have so many questions, Jacob." Eran smiled. "I'm sorry about a lot of things, but I'm mostly sorry for not being able to answer them all."

I waited for them to carry on, and when they didn't, I grew suspicious. "Which memory is this?" I didn't see anyone on the street, anywhere. No young Jacob. None of my parents, or friends. Nothing rang a bell, other than an unnerving sense that I had been there before.

"I don't think this is a memory, Jacob."

"What?" I didn't understand. What else could this be?

"This is the end. Your last station."

They smiled at me with that stupid grin that was barely anything at all. I didn't like it. The pit of my stomach, the hair on my neck, I could not really tell what I was feeling but it made me nervous.

"This is it? This street? What am I supposed to do here?"

Eran just pointed, ever so carefully lifting their arm, toward the blue house right in front of us. "Recognize it?"

"Yeah, kind of, but not really."

"This is in real time. Don't misunderstand, we're still dead and everything. But this is what you're here for."

"Whose house is that?"

"Whose do you think?"

Just as they said it, a painful bubble of air caught in my throat and I knew. I didn't understand what it was that made me realize, but as a cold wave washed over me, the realization was there. "Timmy. From school. He lived there. I was here a few times when we were little, for birthdays and stuff. Maybe once or twice. I don't understand what he has to do with anything?"

"How would you say your life played out?" Eran cocked their head, looking at me like a giant owl.

"Umm . . . not great? I died at twenty. A lot of people see four times as much life as that."

"But with what you had. Are you satisfied?"

I thought back to the memories we had been going through where I had been happy, and I think I smiled. "I can't complain, I guess. I was loved. I had a great family and friends. But, I wish I had more time. I wish I didn't throw it all away and died because I was stupid and careless." A pit began sinking in my stomach. "I wish I achieved something. Wish I'd . . . done something that people could be proud of, you know what I mean?" I thought about my friends. I thought about Ford and Nina. "I wish I had more time with the people who mattered. To grow, to develop myself and my skills." A sour taste rose in the back of my throat. "It's too late now, but yeah I guess I'm satisfied with the little I had."

Eran turned toward the blue house. "How do you think Timmy feels?"

"What do you mean?"

"Remember when you punched him?"

"Yeah, of course. He was an annoying little shit."

"That's how you see it?"

I spread my legs out wide and crossed my arms. I knew it wasn't as one-sided as that. The pit in my stomach grew. "We were kids. That's how it was. I regret it, and it was wrong, but . . ." I took a deep breath. It was surprisingly hard to talk about, even though Eran and I had been through all of this already, even though we had been there and *seen* it. Saying it out loud was hard. "It takes two to tango, you know? He did some things. I did some things. We were both wrong."

Eran walked up to me, turned me around with a surprising strength, and led me through another red door. We were back at school. In the yard, outside. A little bit older than when we had been in woodworking class. My friends and I were standing in a circle around Timmy. We were yelling and arguing, and we took turns pushing Timmy around inside our circle. Eran and I watched as it passed, not stopping before we went through another red door. A football field. Shouting. Arguing. I kicked a ball at Timmy's head. Another red door. George took Timmy's lunch. I laughed. Another red door. Every single time we passed faster and faster, only getting brief glimpses of scenarios where I, Timmy, and our other friends were fighting in some way or other.

Timmy had always been the loud obnoxious one when we were smaller. Eager to fight. Eager to start trouble. But with every single memory, every passing year, he grew smaller and quieter. Weaker and thinner. He went from being the bully to the victim.

"Stop!" I yelled, and the last red door took us back to the street. In front of that blue house that I knew to be Timmy's. My chest was tight and sharp pain pulsed somewhere in my core. It took me a few seconds to realize it was my heart, racing. I buckled over, with my hands on my knees. I would have thrown up if I could.

"Are you still satisfied?"

My back was turned to Eran. My shoulders hunched with the shame. "We didn't — *I* — never meant to bully him."

"Is that an excuse?"

"No." I had to heave for breath. I still wanted to throw up, but I knew I wouldn't be able to. "But it's an explanation. I saw it as revenge. He always used to fight when we were smaller. I took enough shit from him, for years. We all did. It's not my fault I outgrew him. It was about time someone let him have it."

"Starting with that punch in woodworking?" Eran cocked their head in that annoying way he did.

I sighed. "I guess."

"And then you and your friends kept it going. For years."

I finally burst. "I'm sorry!" I yelled as tears sprouted from my eyes. I was still buckled over. My chest still hurt. "I'm sorry, okay? We should have stopped. We should have treated him differently. I . . . what do I do? How do I atone for this? Is this the moment you want me to change? I can go back and not throw the punch, right? I can take it all back!"

When Eran didn't reply, I looked up to see them walking toward the house. "That's up you to decide, Jacob. But I can't guarantee that it will help. Like we've just seen, it doesn't end with just that one punch, even if that started it." They stared up at a small window on the top floor. "Anyway, no matter what you do, Timmy is going to die today."

Those words cut into me like a spear. "What?"

Eran looked at me, and their somber eyes made me understand what they meant. The small window was open just a bit, and the white curtains rustled gently in the breeze. "You can feel it too, right?"

A cold had spread around us. It felt like what mist looks like. It settled in my blood, in my very core. "It's happening right now, isn't it?"

Eran gave me a small nod.

Instinctively, I rushed toward the front door of the house. We couldn't just stand here while my old friend from school died. But Eran spread an arm out, blocking me. It felt like running into a steel beam. Their arm didn't buckle an inch.

"There's nothing you can do to stop it, Jacob. You know you can't interact with anything."

"I can't live with myself knowing I spent my life bullying someone to death!"

"And that's why we're here. You're not living anymore, so you don't have to worry about that. And I'm sorry that you can't change what's happening, but that doesn't mean you won't have a chance to make up for it."

I struggled against their arm, but it was futile. They held me back with ease, while tears still poured from my eyes. "I don't understand!"

"Why do you think we're here?"

"I don't know. Enough with the riddles." It was all too much. I just wanted it to stop.

"Well, try to know. Think about it."

I looked at Eran. Searched their face for clues. My eyes drifted up to stop on the window again. It looked exactly the way I remembered it from when I was little, and then it dawned on me. It felt almost like I had known it the whole time, as if I had planned this very scenario myself through my unconscious guilt.

"I'm his guide. That's why I'm here. I'm the one who has to help him through his moments. To take him through his memories."

Eran smiled, a proper, wide, human smile. "Yes."

"How do I know when to go to him?"

"Whenever you go up there will be his time." Eran turned to look at something behind me, and when I followed their gaze, I saw a purple wooden door in the middle of the street.

"That's my cue," Eran said, nodding toward the door.

Their door.

"Wait! What about my past? I haven't changed anything yet. Isn't that the whole point of this? We've been through my whole life because I was supposed to change, to fix something!"

"Oh, of course." A red door materialized next to their purple. "Take your pick."

I had not expected to be put on the spot like that. Looking back up at Timmy's window, my first instinct was to go back, to not throw that punch. But then I thought about my grandfather, about him lying in the living room when I was out playing. Then, Ford, and the remote flying toward his face. And then, selfishly, I thought about myself. Could I go back and avoid my own death?

"How do I choose?"

"That's the one thing I really can't answer, Jacob."

"What did you choose?"

I think they knew then, that I had realized who they were. There was something in their eyes, a knowing, a hint of a smile on their face.

"I didn't. In the end, it was too hard. I didn't go back to change anything. How could I? There's no way of knowing what might happen. You change the way you act, what you said, did, or how you behaved at a certain time, but who's to say that the outcome changes? Go back and don't punch Timmy, if that makes you feel better Jacob, but will that really stop Timmy from annoying you and your friends for the rest of your school year? Will it stop you from fighting and picking at each other?

"If you don't hurt your brother that one evening in your mom's apartment, will that make you love him more than you already do? I highly doubt that. You're a good kid, Jacob. You have your faults, like everyone else. You get an extra roll of the dice if you feel like you need it, but no one says you have to use it." Eran also looked up at the window, probably knowing what I was thinking. "Chances are, things will play out exactly the same, anyway." They stepped up to their purple door. "Thank you, Jacob. For finally letting me get to know you." They smiled again, a playful, crooked smile. Then the door swung open and Eran stepped through.

"You are *him*, right? I'm not . . . tell me I'm not wrong." I didn't dare say what I was thinking, but Eran hesitated for a moment.

"I am, yes. You got it all figured out, just like I knew you would. I am sorry I had to die so early, when you were so young. We all die for different reasons, Jacob. Not everything is learned in life. What sums us up as people goes well beyond our bodily experiences. I got to come back and guide you. That was my reason, not yours. You get to do some good, for Timmy. And maybe Timmy, who never was good enough, gets to feel like he was."

Eran closed the door and disappeared.

I considered my red door and the blue house in front of me. One last memory to visit before I went to find Timmy. It sounds ironic, but my whole life flashed in front of my eyes just then. Eran was right. I could roll the dice one last time, take a chance. Try not to die. Maybe make some life choice that would make me less careless? But how? Which part of me could I change in just one, single moment?

"I could just play it safe, so to speak. Change nothing, affect no one's life, including my own short-lived one. Accept that it was what it was, I did what I did, and that would have to be my burden. It might be unfair to Timmy, but . . . who was to say what would happen if I changed something? I thought about the butterfly effect. I could change things for the better, or worse. Or it could all turn out exactly the same anyway, like Eran said.

No, I'd gambled enough for one lifetime. An Iron Maiden song hummed somewhere in the back of my mind. I wasn't going to take more risks. I knew which memory I wanted to alter. One that could *only* lead to something good.

I stepped through the red door and opened my eyes to darkness. It was warm and soft all around me and I felt safe.

"I love you, Jacob," I heard my mom whisper as she stroked my hair, kissed my forehead, and stood up from my bed. She put the book she had been reading away on my nightstand and headed toward the door.

"I love you too, Mom," I whispered.

As soon as I said it, I was catapulted through the red door and onto the street. It was done. The perfect memory to change. I got to say it one last time, and Mom got to hear me say it through the darkness as she closed the door to my bedroom. I couldn't think of a better note to end on. Even if it didn't change anything major in the long run.

I looked up at the window in the blue house and headed for the front door.

Stepping through it, I recognized parts of the house, but it also suddenly struck me why Timmy's place wasn't very fresh in my memory. We'd all stopped coming. Birthdays and play dates. We didn't want to go to Timmy's house. Had I not been drenched in it already, I'm sure I would feel shame. His parents were always fighting. His toys were always broken and stupid.

It all came rushing back to me. I'm not sure if it was memories, per se, but a feeling of how we — my friends and I — looked at, talked about, and thought of Timmy.

We excluded him. He distanced himself. Stopped coming to class. I think the last I heard, his dad left them. His mom was on benefits. His older sister moved across the country to go to college. I don't remember ever hearing anything about her coming back to visit.

I walked in through the front hall. It was dark. Dim bulbs

lit up rooms that looked exactly the same as when we were little. Maybe the color had changed, but I didn't think so.

Somehow, I knew exactly where to go. Upstairs. That red door. The red wooden door I had been seeing everywhere but never recognized. I had passed it several times when I was little, when I had headed up these stairs on my way to Timmy's room. It was his door. Not back then, but now. The master bedroom.

It was partially open.

I took a deep breath.

Let's go.

He stood there, in the middle of the room looking down at his bed. He looked a bit rough. Drawn face, stubble lining his face. He looked to be in good shape, but maybe not because he worked out a lot and ate healthy, more because he was worn out. Thin, almost. His hair was beginning to crawl back toward the top of his head, and I realized he was older than I was when I died. Maybe ten years older, fifteen perhaps. He wore a nice shirt. Definitely more expensive than anything I had ever worn. His shoes were black and shiny, looking like he had just finished polishing them.

I almost teared up again.

The bedroom was nice, I realized as I looked around. Tidy and well-kept, with a made bed and expensive pillows. I couldn't be certain, but it looked like he maybe shared it with someone.

His body lay there, looking like he was simply sleeping.

I turned briefly to look out through the doorway I'd come through on my way up the stairs. What else had I missed in Timmy's old childhood home? Was the downstairs as nice as this?

I turned back and for the first time Timmy noticed me. He had a confused look on his face, one I recognized immediately.

There's something curious about looking at your dead body in your own bed. You know it should freak you out, but at the same time, you can't look away. He didn't freak out when he saw me either. Being dead will do that to you.

"Who are you?" he asked, with that careful voice I had forgotten.

I thought about it for what seemed like ages, but I'm guessing no more than a second passed. I wanted to smile wide, but I stopped myself. I did not want to be the first one in a long line of guides to break the character.

"Eran," I said, holding back a grin.

"Where am I?"

I knew he knew he was in his home of course, but that's not what he was asking.

"You're dead, Timmy. But don't worry. I'll take care of you."

Acknowledgements

As always, there are many people to thank when I finish a book. First of all, thanks to Dakota Rayne, and everyone else at Inked In Gray, for believing in my vision and for all the care they took to make this story as great as it is. It wouldn't have been the same without you.

Thanks to my friends in the writing community, one I have mostly been a part of online, but where I've made many dear friends. Thanks particularly to David Gane, who's been a mentor.

Thanks to Benjamin Brown, who never fails to be interested in my creative endeavors. Being able to always come to you with ideas, problems, and stories to discuss is always helpful.

Thanks to my mother, father, two sisters (whom I unfairly merged into one character) and my little brother, both for the inspiration and the encouragement.

And finally – always – thanks to Maria. You make me believe in myself in a way that would be impossible alone.

About Trey Stone

Trey Stone has studied archaeology in England, excavated burial sites in the Arctic, and has more guitars than underwear. He grew up on a farm in western Norway, and has a bunch of siblings, half-siblings, in-laws, and is uncle to *at least* nineteen kids. They're all pretty awesome, as far as he knows. It's difficult to remember who's who anymore.

Trey has been telling stories for as long as he can remember, and when he's not writing books or short stories, he enjoys playing guitar, hiking, and playing old video games. He currently live in Svalbard, where he enjoys the midnight sun and the polar night with his wife.

Trey Stone is also the author of *At The Gate*, *A Form Of Revenge,* **A State of Despair** and **The Consequence of Loyalty**. In his native Norwegian he's written *Fjordbeist*. You can find Trey on Amazon, Goodreads, and Twitter, or **on his website**.

Also by Trey Stone

If you enjoyed *A Death Worth Living*, please consider also reading *At The Gate*, also by Trey Stone or any of the other Inked in Gray novels and anthologies. Support our small business by buying direct at InkedinGray.com

We also appreciate any and all reviews! You may leave a review on Goodreads, Amazon, IndieStoryGeek or on our site at Inkedingray.com